In the Shadow
of the Wind

Translated by Sheila Fischman

In the Shadow of the Wind

Anne Hébert

Stoddart/*Toronto*
A member of the General Publishing Group

First published by Editions du Seuil
Copyright © 1982 Editions du Seuil
English translation copyright © 1983 Stoddart Publishing

This translation was assisted by a grant from the Canada Council.

First published in English in Canada by Stoddart,
a division of General Publishing Co. Limited,
30 Lesmill Road,
Don Mills, Ontario,
M3B 2T6

CANADIAN CATALOGUING IN PUBLICATION DATA

Hébert, Anne, 1916-
[Les Fous de Bassan.   English]
In the shadow of the wind

Translation of: Les Fous de Bassan.
ISBN 0-7737-2016-2

1. Title.   II. Title: Les Fous de Bassan.   English.
PS8515.E16F6813   C843'.54   C83-098681-2
PQ3919.H37F6813

Printed and bound in the United States

NOTE TO THE READER

ALL MY RECOLLECTIONS of the north shore and the south shore of the St. Lawrence River, and of the Gulf and the islands, have been blended together and turned over to my imagination, where they have become a single place called Griffin Creek, located between Cap Sec and Cap Sauvagine. A fictional place between the city of Quebec and the Atlantic Ocean, the site of a story that bears no relation to any actual event that might have occurred.

THE BOOK OF THE REVEREND NICHOLAS JONES

Autumn 1982

Ye are the salt of the earth: but
if the salt have lost his savor,
wherewith shall it be salted?

St. Matthew

A STRAND OF sea poised between tides, white, as far as the eye can see, and against the gray sky, in a parallel line behind us, the black bulk of trees.

In the distance, from the new village, the hum of festivities. If you craned your neck you could see their shacks, daubed with red, green, yellow, blue, as if they took pleasure in smearing houses with garish colors. They're upstarts, those people. Unnecessary to look in their direction. I know they're there.

Their brass band is drowned by the wind. I hear spurts of music. Earsplitting. Glittering, savage and strident. They have bought up our lands as they reverted to the Crown. Papists. Today, with quantities of instruments and majorettes, they dare to celebrate the country's bicentennial as if they were the ones who had founded it, built it, they who first came to the forest, the sea, they who had broken the virgin soil with their plows.

It took just one summer to disperse the chosen people of Griffin Creek. A few survivors still hang on, dragging themselves from church to house, from house to outbuildings. Sturdy generations of prolific Loyalists who would end up here, finish and dissolve into nothingness, their offspring now old and without issue. Our houses are falling into decay where they stand and I, Nicholas Jones, minister without a flock, languish in this rectory with its worm-eaten gray pillars.

In the beginning there was only taiga, here on the edge of the sea between Cap Sec and Cap Sauvagine. All animals with feathers or fur, with white flesh or dark, the birds of the sea and the fish of the water multiplied therein, to infinity.

And the Spirit of God moved upon the face of the waters.

Cast out onto the road from New England, men, women, and children faithful to a mad king, turning their backs on American independence, received from the Canadian government grants of land, the right to hunt and fish. Joneses, Browns, Atkinses, Macdonalds. Their names can be seen on the tombstones in the little graveyard that overlooks the sea.

I, Nicholas Jones, son of Peter Jones and Felicity Brown, after facing for long days and nights the ruin of Griffin Creek, hit upon the idea of building an annex to the rectory, where I would set up a gallery of ancestors so as to proclaim that my blood would endure. Twenty feet by fifteen, wood, fitted together carefully like a square box the color of fresh wood-shavings. I sent the twin daughters of John and Bea Brown to the new village, to buy paint and brushes. I looked at myself closely in the mirror, the remnant of a disappearing tribe, and beginning with my own disquieting face I went back to the source, back to 1782.

I am short-legged and sturdy, with a square jaw and a large head, my hair, once red, now overgrown with white strands. On the back of my skull, a thinner patch, yellow like snow. Ravaged features. This man, shattered so long ago, goes on as if nothing had happened.

In my own image and likeness I beget my father, who begets my grandfather in his image and likeness, and so on to the first image and likeness, counting all the way back to the Joneses who came to Griffin Creek in 1782. I who had no sons beget my fathers unto the tenth generation. I who am without issue am pleased to restore my ancestors to this world, back to the very first, to the face of Henry Jones, born in Montpelier, Vermont.

I paint on beaverboard, first coated with colorless shellac. In black suits and white linen my ancestors loom into sight like the flat figures on playing cards. Identical, interchangeable, their hair going from red to blond, changing to chestnut, they hang on the wall of the portrait gallery. Round eyes, crooked noses, naive and terrible. Rough-hewn hands.

If you walk past them somewhat quickly, you feel you are being followed, from one board to the next, by the same gimlet eyes.

For the women, I decided to resort to the twins. Let daughters give birth to mothers, all the way back to 1782, when the first creature in petticoats left her light footprint on the shore of Griffin Creek. Set loose with brushes and paint, shut away in the portrait gallery for a whole day, the twins have slathered the walls with cascades of lace, with flounces, checks and dots and multicolored stripes, with flowers, leaves, red birds, blue fish, crimson seaweed. A few heads of women emerge from it all, wearing hats, quills, ribbons, some with only one eye or lacking a nose or mouth, and more alive than any dream creature who has haunted Griffin Creek since the mists of time.

Turning chronology upside down, inventing for themselves grandmothers and sisters galore, the twins discover the pleasure of painting. Spattered with colors from head to toe, they go into raptures before their creations. And take malicious pleasure, though I've expressly forbidden it, in causing the Atkins girls and Irene, my wife, to appear several times on the wall. Three women's heads drift upon a sea-green background covered with waterweeds, fishnets, ropes and stones. Three women's names, spelled out in black letters, are flung here and there, at the bottom of the painting, at the top, on the right, the left, or crosswise; they merge with the wild grasses, are inscribed on a pale brow or carved into a round cheek, like a gash. Over and over, in sparkling letters formed with care, Nora, Olivia, Irene, they dance before my eyes, as I walk through the room. As for the coal-black garland, patiently worked and unfurled all along the baseboard, if you bend down and look carefully you can distinguish the numbers, always the same ones, joined together in a single endless graffiti: 1936193619361936193619361936. Lower down, in smaller characters, a second line, just as regular and obstinate, indecipherable at first:

summersummersummersummersum-
mersummersummersummer

A whole wall spoiled. The very idea of the gallery sabo-
taged, devastated. I shouldn't have let the twins set loose their
imaginations in the ancestors' gallery. They're mad, those
girls. Not total idiots like their brother Percival, nor evil like
their other brother, Stevens, but crazy all the same. Behave
foolishly. With their heads filled with insane imagery that
runs wild on my walls. Those girls are haunted. It runs in
the family. I took them into my service long ago, their bodies
still uncertain and their souls indistinct, with blonde braids
and stifled laughter. Maintained them, body and soul, in that
malleable state, without taking into account the passage of
time. Time slips over them like water off a duck's back. Without ever having been women, now they are suffering the
change of life with the same look of astonishment as their
first periods. Not an ounce of fat, neither breasts nor hips,
slender skeletons of birds. I have taught them to live frugally,
in the fear of my displeasure. I like to see them tremble when
I reprimand them, in the kitchen filled with steam and the
lingering odor of boiled linen. Everything here is washed and
soaped daily, as if to erase a constantly recurring stain.

*Sin lieth at the door. And unto thee shall be his desire, and thou
shalt rule over him.*

I have shut up the ancestors' gallery, forbidden the twins
to return there. Their crumpled little faces, their obstinate
expressions. They lower their heads, eyes filled with tears.
Beg to be given their brushes and poster paint. Ever since *I
say to this woman, Go, and she goeth; and to the other, Come, and
she cometh*, I am surprised at their sudden protests.

Autumn. Whenever the door is opened, the smell of rotting
leaves enters the kitchen along with waves of dark and cold.
Huddled together, the lights of the new village sparkle in the
night. Through the wet trees, music can be heard.

The twins' slender braids wound around their heads. No
way of knowing if there are white hairs among the blonde.
Those silvery, almost lunar glints have always been there. I
call them "my angel" and "my dove," but most of the time I
bully them. Never touching them, using only my cavernous
bass voice, I turn them over like light leaves in the wind. For

them alone, I spout my finest sermons. All the angels in heaven, all the demons in hell surge from the Bible in answer to my call, hastening at night to the bedside of the sleeping twins. Fed on Scripture, on prophets and kings, the twins dream fierce and glorious dreams. I, the master of their daydreams, have a pathetic ministry, small in scale. But my authority is absolute.

And the Word was made flesh and dwelt among us.

One day I was the Word of Griffin Creek, guardian of the Word at Griffin Creek, myself the Word amid the faithful, who were silent through strength, unpolished by nature and gathered together in the little wooden church.

Accustomed by their parents to obedience from earliest childhood, they have been serving me for almost forty-six years. Their father and mother having wished, very early, to lose them in the forest, they quite simply turned the twins over to me, when they were thirteen.

They have scrawled summer193619361936 in precise, regular characters all along the baseboard in the ancestors' gallery.

My little servants delight in each other as in two perfect mirrors. As soon as my back is turned, the twins return to their twins' secrets, to their muffled laughter, their chuckles, and furtive caresses. Sleep at night in one another's arms.

"I'm Pam."

"I'm Pat."

They reply when I ask which is which. Laugh at my confusion. Enjoy misleading me. Identical, interchangeable, until a burn left a mark on Pat's wrist. Since then, I need only check the pearly scar to know which one I'm dealing with. By thus discouraging any vague desire for trickery on the part of the twins, I have taken advantage of the situation to reinforce my own authority. I call them by name, and they obey me.

I have dwelt among them and I was one of them, the Joneses, the Browns, the Atkinses, the Macdonalds. All the same, a link is missing in the chain of men in the ancestors' gallery. After me, an abrupt chasm. The void. Nothing. How am I to imagine the face of the son I never had, the breadth of his shoulders, the strength of his hands, his soul tormented by the strangeness of the world?

The noise of dishes, endless. Glasses clink. Plates clatter against the sink. Must tell the twins not to make such a racket. Once again, too much soap in the wash water. They plunge their arms in the suds up to the elbows. For a joke. Send them to bed straightaway. But first, ask them to get my pipes ready for the evening. I like them well cured, already filled and lined up on the table ready to be lit, hour after hour, according to a very precise ritual. Thus passeth the minister's evening, punctuated by fiery pipes and Bible reading, until midnight. Woe to him who is without liturgy, who is sunk in a solitude comparable to mine, in a night as dark as mine.

Now they are scouring the sink with Old Dutch. There's no end to their racket. Pale locks fall onto their noses in the steam rising from the hot water. I'll send them to bed right away. Their good nights, murmured through extremely small and pointed teeth, remind me of the drooling mouth of their brother Percival, an inmate at Baie Saint-Paul. Though he caused quite a stir on the shore of Griffin Creek all one summer. Knew everything but could only howl. Had no words for what he knew. Like a dog howling at death. Shortly after August 31 his parents had him put away. John and Bea Brown, having given birth to Stevens, Percival, and the twins, got rid of them all in the course of a single summer. An old dream finally come true, and justified. To be utterly childless. To be simply husband and wife, as before. Facing one another. China dogs for all eternity. With no witnesses.

The first pipe sends thick wreaths up to the ceiling. Through half-shut eyes I see the twins take off their aprons and hang them on a nail behind the kitchen door. I close one eye. Two scrawny silhouettes go past my open eye. Not interested enough to look for the scar on . . . whose wrist? No identification possible. Too tired. Never mind. Shut the open eye. Open the one that was closed. See again the twins' wiry legs as they climb the stairs, one behind the other. The third step and the sixth one creak, as usual.

I struggle out of the kitchen, awash in tobacco smoke. The thick cloud accompanies me into the parlor, follows me to my high-backed armchair. Small straw-bottomed chairs, books on boards, a potbellied roll-top desk. The Epistle of Paul, the Gospel According to St. John close to hand, as if one could feel the apostles breathe merely by touching the black-leather binding. My consecrated hands. One day . . . *The Lord is my shepherd*. For how long? *That is the question*. Outside, the rustling of insects erupts in the night, wrapping the house in a murmuring blanket. While something strange is going on inside the room where I am riveted to my chair. It's as if my blood is pounding outside of me, rapping against walls and beams. A muffled rumble, a throbbing. How long shall I be able to bear it?

I lean against the arms of my chair. Make two attempts to rise. That weakness in the small of my back. The control levers don't respond. Fear for my old bones lost in the heavy mass of my flesh. I get to my feet. Hear once more the sound of my heart filling the room that's covered with tattered blue wallpaper. I call out.

I awaken the twins. From the foot of the stairs, my hands cupped around my mouth, I scream,

"Pat! Pam!"

Eyes swollen, braids undone, the old little girls shiver in their nightgowns. I make a fuss about a long blonde hair I've found on the kitchen table. Anger is good for me. Calms me completely. I send them back to bed.

The blue wallpaper in the parlor is in shreds, revealing, in places, the brown skin of wood, stained with glue. Under the pressure of my fingers I feel once more the familiar heartbeat at my wrist. One of the twins declares that termites are eating away at the house, that one day we will have to sweep up the ceilings and walls, reduced to sawdust.

With the twins back in bed, I settle firmly again in my arm-chair. The Epistles and the Apocalypse close at hand. The present has hardly any purchase on my soul now. I am an old man who hears voices, perceives vanished colors and forms.

Summersummersummer 193619361936 the twins have written in black poster paint all along the baseboard in the portrait gallery.

In those times . . .

My wife Irene, née Macdonald, is barren. In other places, under other laws, I would have repudiated her openly and publicly as a useless creature.

But this I say, brethren, the time is short: it remaineth, that both they that have wives be as though they had none.

She sleeps against me in the big bed like a dead fish, her existence as cold as a fish, her fish eye under the lid without lashes, the fishy odor when I insist on seeking between her thighs, a child, pleasure.

Great migratory birds in close formation pass over Griffin Creek, casting their black shadow over the rectory. I hear distant barking, hounds of heaven moving away in the night.

Shall I once more rub my nose in my sin? Admit that as I lie against Irene's sleeping body, moments after folding my ecclesiastical garment on a chair at the foot of the bed, I secretly weigh in my hands the slight weight, the delicate forms of the Atkins girls?

Let every man abide in the same calling wherein he was called.

That should not have been written four centuries ago, and the words addressed to the Corinthians left to make their way through time and space to me, Nicholas Jones, son of Peter Jones and Felicity, née Brown, legitimate descendants of Henry Jones and Maria Brown, both of them washed up on the shore of Griffin Creek one day in June 1782, fleeing the American Revolution.

Unable to avoid God, I became a minister, like one who sees God before him and advances through dense clouds. The will of God upon me. The desire of God. The mark of the lamb on my brow. The indelible feature. I did not have to choose. I was chosen. Appointed, called, out of all those from Griffin Creek, to accomplish the work of the Lord.

When I was twelve years old I confided to my mother the secret of my vocation, talking into her ear which was uncovered by her pulled-back hair.

She kisses me for the first time. Her face salty as spindrift. A tear on her cheek. My mother's long neck. Her stiff collar. Her black bodice stuck with pins where I, a child, dare not lay my head. Underneath it, the warmth of her life that throbs, throbs like a captive bird. And if I were to open the cage? What magic prayer, what invention of mad love would let me free my mother's heart? I dream of it as of some impossible mission. Am ecstatic if Felicity's hand grazes mine.

I learn the psalms of David by heart. Recite them as I stand on a rock overlooking the sea. I address the water, want to talk louder than it, convince it of my power and strength. Tame it utterly. Charm it to its very depths. I try out my voice on the sea. One day I shall give sermons and address the people of Griffin Creek gathered together in the little wooden church. For the moment, I cast the words of David out over the waves. It is as if the wind breaks the crests of the waves into wild scattered plumes. Only the cries of the seabirds touch the water so closely, scoring it with a luminous beam. Let him who has received the duty of the word use it upon the surface of the waters, let him utter his clamor and send intelligent, resonant chants into the wind. I will make you fishers of men, saith the Lord, the mass of the faithful shall be before you, not just this rim of foaming water.

Therefore is my spirit overwhelmed within me; my heart within me is desolate.

Throughout this story you must never lose sight of the wind, of the presence of the wind, its keen voice in our ears, its salty breath on our lips. No act is performed by man or woman in this land that is not accompanied by the wind. Hair, dresses, shirts, trousers clatter in the wind, upon bare bodies. The sea's breath enters our clothing, uncovers our salt-glazed breasts. Our porous souls are pierced straight through. The wind here has always blown too hard and what took place was possible only because of the wind, the maddening, intoxicating wind.

I must caulk the windows, stop up the chinks between the planks, close the parlor like a fist, once again stop the wind from . . . I shall tell Pam and Pat to buy caulking. Already I hear them saying that the windows in this house are moldy, that it's useless to . . .

I light my third pipe. The amber tip in my mouth, like sucking a too-hard nipple. Since the time when . . . I'm an old man exhausted with living. I'll tell Pat and Pam to stop up the windows. I'm afraid of mildew. If it's not the wind it's the rain, or both at once. An icy draft slips down between my shoulders. Rivulets on the floor, blackish rings on kitchen and bedroom walls. Corrosion by salt. Slow vegetable fermentation. One day the entire house will crumble with the soft thud of rotten wood.

And they that use this world, as not abusing it: for the fashion of this world passeth away. The land, the sky, the water of Griffin Creek will pass like a dream but I, saith the Lord, I shall not pass. To be certain of that and die in the light of the Word. Never will such certainty be given me, nor death so violent and fast. My slow disintegration in this worm-eaten dwelling, while behind me the forest creeps closer each day, each night, planting new shoots of birch and spruce under my very windows. If I dare to open them in the night and try to discover the secret of my imminent end, I breathe deep of the odor of gravid earth and it catches at my throat.

The fourth pipe burns my tongue and stings my eyes. Concealed by its smoke like a cuttlefish in its ink, I examine my soul and seek the original sin of Griffin Creek. No, Stevens was not the first one to fail, though he is the worst of us all, the guardian of all the secret evil done in Griffin Creek and stored away in the hearts of its men and and its women for two hundred years.

I see the faithful in their Sunday best, crammed together in the little wooden church, the women in bright dresses, the men in black suits, macerating in their everyday odor, slightly musky in the July heat. Unpolished, they speak seldom and what they say is banal. The poetry of the Word enters their hearts by surprise. I, master of Holy Writ, speak to them in the name of God. For some time now I have been choosing the Sunday psalms and hymns with special care, thinking of the Atkins girls. Their eyes, violet and ultramarine, are raised up to me, for my damnation. They sing and pray, they appropriate the words of the apostles and prophets, their child-like souls take on maturity and form in the splendor of Holy Writ. I prepare them as if they were young women betrothed, attentive to the love song that is coming toward them in the summer light. I modulate, enunciate each sound, each syllable, turning the breath of the earth into the word of God.

Thou hast ravished my heart with one hair of thy neck.

The Song of Songs grips the wise and silent heart of Olivia Atkins, flushing out words that should never have departed the sober, silent night of Olivia Atkins. Her violet eyes. She lifts her head to me. Her beautiful face. *One hair of thy neck,* she thinks, looking toward me but not seeing me, lit from inside as by a bright lamp. Turns around now (feeling eyes on her back), toward the door of the church, wide open to the luminous yellow summer, the sea itself luminous in the distance, green with silver curls. Looks at Stevens. Is looked at by him.

He, with his back to the light, stands firmly on his long legs in the doorway, a dark determined gangling silhouette suffused with sunlight from head to toe, refusing to enter, refusing to join us, refusing to share our songs and our prayer. His emaciated face, his pale eyes in the shadow of his dark brown hat. He seems to be looking for someone among the faithful who have gathered together for Sunday worship.

The smoke here is thick enough to cut with a knife. Stifling. I'll call the twins to open the window. I'm wedged too deep in this chair. Hindquarters like lead. The window on the other side of the table. Too far. Reach for the bell on the table. Once again. Call the twins. Snatch them from sleep as if they were a single person. Tell them to open the window. As long as they've been in my service. Must be prepared to appear before me at the slightest call. I shake the bell as hard as I can. My little servant girls are sound sleepers.

The harmonium pours waves of sound out the door of the church, opened wide at the height of noon. The whole countryside streaming with light vibrates and sings, starting at the church in Griffin Creek. Nasal voices drone away.

My soul exults in the Lord.

Voices, only voices, sounds, only sounds. I light another pipe, ears filled with the music of bygone days, with shrill voices. Above all not to hear again the sermon of the Reverend Nicholas Jones, who coos and rejoices at the sound of his own voice.

My son is listening to himself talk, thinks Felicity Jones as the trembling sun leaves bright spots on her joined hands.

Uncle Nicholas is talking about God, thinks Nora Atkins, but for some time now I haven't heard the word of God in my uncle's voice. It's as if God had disappeared from my uncle's voice. My uncle's resonant voice has no piety in it, my uncle's voice as beautiful as a gleaming shell, devoid of content, virile and bass, fluid as smoke. I like the sound of his male voice in the little church.

If it's true that I use my voice dramatically for that little girl who has barely left childhood behind, it's because she resembles me and I resemble her. The two reddest heads in Griffin Creek, lustrous as foxes, Percival declares. God having pulled us both, despite the difference in age, from the same warm carnal earth.

I pay attention to my oratorical gestures. Round them off in the summer light. My sturdy freckled hands. Nora's attention is extreme, as if she were gazing at a fly in flight. But now it is she who turns her head toward the back of the church. Stevens stands there, dark in the light. His hat on his head. Stevens looking at Nora now. Nora looking at Stevens.

A slight bustle among the faithful. Heads swivel in the direction of the open door and the yellow sun. Stevens turns on his heel and disappears. Seen by them all. Examined, weighed, and judged by them all.

Too close to one another. Those people are never alone. They hear each other breathing. Can't move their little finger without their neighbor knowing. Their most secret thoughts are snatched at the source, very quickly no longer belong to them, haven't time to become words.

Stevens should never have come back to us.

I murmur the words they expect of me. That praise, that exaltation of themselves, of their vocation as a chosen people in a savage land, face to the sea, back to the mountain.

The children of Israel were fruitful, and increased abundantly, and multiplied, and waxed exceedingly mighty; and the land was filled with them.

And the gathering of the faithful stands and faces me, Nicholas Jones, mute and contemplative. The Joneses, the Browns, the Atkinses, and the Macdonalds.

I finish the Sunday sermon in the greatest confusion. A hasty sign of the cross. I hear my heart beating. I beseech the peace of the Lord.

Since the service started, Percival has been staring at his cousins Nora and Olivia. A single legendary animal, he thinks, with two heads, two bodies, four legs, and four arms, made for adoration or massacre. Percival wipes his watery eyes, his drooling mouth. Deep in contemplation of his huge hands.

It is good for a man not to touch a woman. Nevertheless, to avoid fornication, let every man have his own wife, and let every woman have her own husband.

Irene's broad, flat face, with no wrinkle, no sign of laughter or weeping, smooth, ageless: one might think it eternal. Her modest expression, née Macdonald. Her hollow stare. Reassuring, at first glance. Cut out to be a minister's wife, a gray shadow behind the minister's sacred person.

It is better to marry than to burn.

If only Irene, my wife, would give me a son I could offer to my mother, Felicity Jones, as evidence of my potency. I am certain my son would quickly become my mother's favorite, the apple of her eye as I never was. She will rock him in her sturdy arms, against the gentle warmth of her bosom, and I shall be restored to grace. My son will soon supplant the Atkins girls in the heart of Felicity Jones, in my name and my stead.

The parlor is full of bluish smoke. Like an aquarium filled with thick swirls of capricious water. The smell of tobacco rises to the ceiling, in flaccid waves. Breathe inside it. Absorb it through the skin's pores, through the warp and weft of my clothing, saturating the hair on head and body, burning eyes and throat. I am standing now, leaning against the back of my armchair. No more than two steps to take. The window's there, on my left. Open it to the damp night. Let the house exhale all its tobacco-tainted breath through the open window. The surrounding trees draw closer, with their moist respiration, their odor of resin and sap. The boards of the house moan like forest trees. Somewhere deep in the forest, living trees answer the dead trees of the house. The somber night is filled with the call of trees and of vegetation advancing in triumph toward the rotten heart of this dwelling.

While from the sea, glowing salt and foam push forward, victorious, and lap at the sand. In a few hours, with the sun, the tide will be high.

Call the twins. Before dawn breaks over the sea. Above all, I must not be surprised by the images of ancient dawn. I'll take advantage of the black night to burrow into black sleep. My shoulders shudder. I must have caught cold. It's freezing here with the window open. I shout at them to come down. Sense the twins' mocking presence. It's enough. I wish they'd look after me. Bring my slippers and pyjamas. Shut the window. Support me, at arms' length, as I ascend the stairs. Their dry little hands on the small of my back. Their rapid breathing.

Scraps of voices. Pealing bell. Again and again, the ringing bell.

Barefoot, ill at ease in her long nightgown, one of the twins slowly descends the stairs. Sleepwalking. Yawns, rubs her eyes. An old little girl. A blade of grass, a pin, an ant. Insignificant. A nondescript object—animal, vegetable—torn from sleep, one of hundreds of animal-vegetable objects, identical, interchangeable, lost in sleep. I look for the mark on her wrist. "Pat?" I say. She shakes her head. Curls her upper lip over her small teeth. Desolate grimace that serves as a smile. Drunk with sleep, she enjoys taking advantage of me. Repeats, "Pam? Pat?" in a confused manner. Raises misty eyes at me.

After just heating some milk in the kitchen, which she brings to me in a steaming bowl, she falls and now sleeps at my feet. The bowl caught in mid-flight. I sip. The urge to nudge the heap of white cloth collapsed on the rag rug with my foot.

The foamy milk fills my mouth with sweet warmth. Will I fall asleep in the sweetness of the milk? Go back to the world's warm beginnings? What sort of wishful thinking is that? Drop the box of matches at the foot of the sleeping twin. The last of the milk sipped from the bottom of the bowl. Then nothing. No pipe. No milk. Utter deprivation. Emptiness. My mouth grimaces like a goldfish blowing bubbles. This man is old, grotesque, too fat, he opens and closes his mouth as if he were suckling.

With no tear or cry Felicity Jones gives birth to sons and daughters according to her husband's pleasure. Without fuss or reproaches. Felicity Jones feigns ignorance of her husband's escapades. Increasingly resembles an offended queen. Escapes into the dawn, weather permitting. In her old dressing gown with a dark-brown-and-red pattern of leaves, Felicity rushes onto the beach, like someone keeping an appointment.

She has chosen this indistinct hour between day and night to escape while the males of her blood sway behind her, in the house shut up deep in sleep. A scant hour of solitude (far removed from conjugal and household tasks), her hands idle, feet bare on the sand, staring out at the gray sea, her heart released from all its knots of pride and virtue; loving and hating in peace, in the morning calm.

And I, Nicholas Jones, am a mere child awakening amid the sleeping breath of father and children. Behind the fir wall I make out Felicity's muffled commotion in the dark. Sheets thrown back, a stifled yawn, a nightgown rustling against bare skin. I hear my father snoring. Soon my mother will be ready, in her old dressing gown and her desire for solitude. The kitchen door opens and shuts, heavy with oil and silence. The son slips into the shadow of his mother, as the door shuts silently, crosses the sandy road, tumbles down the path, feels the nocturnal coolness of the beach under his bare feet.

Hidden in the reeds, I watch the sun rise over the sea. Felicity Jones is awash in pink glimmers. When the tide allows it, she advances into the icy water. Her legs push aside the rose-colored water and rounds of color move about her ankles, encircle them like bracelets, ever larger and looser. Felicity floats on her back. Spreads her arms and legs like a star. She reigns over the sea. Her dressing gown with its brown-and-red pattern of leaves drifts about her. Like a giant medusa.

The light trembles like mist above the sea. Felicity emerges from the water, straightens her dressing gown. There is a spot on her right shoulder the color of milky coffee. And I who am so small on the sand and she, so tall, I hop around her like a grasshopper. I plead.

"Take me, take me swimming with you."

My mother says no gently, as if awakening from a dream. A dream's reflection still hovers on her face, peaceful now, it lingers at the corners of her lips, so that she seems to be emerging from a joyous mystery. Takes my hand. Her cold hand, wet, in mine. Leads me back to the house.

"Bring me with you tomorrow."

She shakes her head again. Scowls slightly. Then her face becomes all concern, as we walk up the front steps.

"Get right into bed now, or you'll catch cold."

Her back is already turned when I hear her voice through the thickness of her back, the confused voice of a woman betrayed, as if she were speaking to no one.

"Your father came in at three o'clock this morning."

Back in the warmth of my bed, I fall asleep amid the familiar sounds of the kitchen gradually awakening, under the orders of Felicity Jones, my mother, my love.

The Atkins girls *being not yet born, neither having done any good or evil, that the purpose of God according to election might stand, not of works, but of him that calleth.* Felicity will offer love only when her granddaughters come into the world.

Time works for my mother and against my father. Peter Jones very quickly comes undone, growing fat almost as we watch, soon he walks potbellied, pees crooked, groans, and hardly ever leaves the house. No longer fearing her husband's insults, Felicity is approaching a grandmother's age like someone who is just starting to live. She who had eyes not to see and ears not to hear (too outraged by that from the first year of her marriage) is beginning to gaze upon the pink fields of fireweed, the golden fields of ripe oats, the fields of new-mown buckwheat where long red streaks still linger. The sea, whose tides, faithful or faithless, she no longer experiences within her body, lulls her at daybreak and makes her sharper than salt. Felicity Jones adores her grandchildren and her grandchildren adore her. I think she has always preferred girls. And as for her daughters' daughters, her satisfaction knows no bounds. Olivia Atkins, daughter of Matilda Jones and Philip Atkins, Nora Atkins, daughter of Alice Jones and Ben Atkins, double first cousins, sisters almost, the final jewels in a line of obscure women.

NoraOliviaNoraOlivia the twins have written on the walls in the portrait gallery. Eyes of violet and ultramarine. Pale masks on vacant faces. Too fanciful. I shouldn't have put paints and brushes in the hands of the twins (these girls are mad), shouldn't have entrusted these vanished faces to them.

The one who was asleep at my feet, a little bundle of sticks buried inside a loose nightgown, has got to her feet without my noticing, probably to go back to the warm bed she shares with her sister. I should have kept her here. Told her to pick up the box of matches. To erase her imaginings from the walls of the portrait gallery. Perhaps insist that she rub my shoulders. Urge her to bring a rug for my knees. It's freezing in this shack. The solitude of the wet night. The night's dark silence, like human breath.

It took only one summer, one of those brief summers we have here, whittled down at both ends by the frost, it took scarcely two months for Nora and Olivia Atkins to leave childhood behind, to take charge of their slight age and disappear on the shore of Griffin Creek, on the evening,of August 31, 1936.

Their descriptions will be broadcast on every Canadian and American radio station.

Blessed is he that watcheth, and keepeth his garments, lest he walk naked, and they see his shame.

Wearing his black suit and clerical collar, his face reddened by the wind, the Reverend Nicholas Jones scales the dunes, crosses the sandbar with its lacy edge of black and violet seaweed cast up by the tide, and with one hand shielding his eyes, pretends to look at the horizon.

Reeds creak in the wind, bow down then right themselves, long tangled tufts, bright green, almost white. This place is inhabited by a thousand lives, visible and invisible. The Reverend Jones has never been alone here, not even when he thought he was peacefully watching Felicity Jones's favorite granddaughters frolic in the icy water with their grandmother, at dawn. Percival is already there, hidden in the rushes quite close to the minister, breathing hard, staring wide-eyed out to sea, on the verge of tears.

The red globe of the sun climbs to the horizon amid the screeching of sea birds. In snowy bands the gannets leave their nest on the summit of the cliff, plunge vertically into the sea, pointed at beak and tail like knives, send up sprays of foam. Shouts and sharp laughter mingle with the wind, with the heart-rending clamor of the birds. Occasionally words come loose, skip off the water like stones.

"Cold! Cold!"

"Good Lord!"

"I'm freezing!"

"It's killing me!"

"I'm turning to ice! Worse than yesterday!"

"Freezing!"

Felicity floats on her back. Nora and Olivia try to swim,

imitating the rapid movements of dogs struggling in the water. Soon they can be seen dancing on the sand to warm themselves. Their wet hair molds the smooth little skulls, woolen bathing suits cling to their adolescent bodies. Wanting to touch with his puppy's paws his cousins streaming with water, and afraid of being punished for it, Percival weeps utterly.

The minister walks away, with long strides, enjoys bursting with his heels the swollen yellow sea-plants.

Knowing this, that our old man is crucified with him, that the body of sin might be destroyed, that henceforth we should not serve sin.

It is not easy to chase the old man away, he is here now, persistent, embedded in me like a tick, between flesh and hide. I would like to cling to the present, feel the burning bowl of my pipe in my numb fingers. No use trying to pick up the box of matches that fell to the rug at my feet. Out of reach. Arms too short. Back doesn't bend. Stiff neck. The night is pitiless and propitious to apparitions.

Hairy and evil, rifles over their shoulders, the men around here always seem to want to kill some living creature. Their houses are full of hunting trophies. Deer and moose seem to be sticking their stupefied heads through the walls, in the silent rooms. The sheds are littered with snares and well-oiled traps with powerful teeth. Houses overflow with guns and knives, carefully polished during long winter evenings. Home from the hunt, they take their wives in the dark, without removing their boots. Out of season, ropes and weights for the salmon-fishing nets lie in the boathouses in heaps. I, Nicholas Jones, pastor of Griffin Creek, can attest to a salmon that took two hours to die, at the end of my line. The sea is red with blood.

Called by God, pulled from the silt of Griffin Creek by God, to accomplish the perfect image of the lamb within my soul, in the most secret hollow of my bones, I return endlessly now to the primeval earth and I am one with them, my hard and savage brothers.

The calamity of Griffin Creek is before me, between Cap Sec and Cap Sauvagine.

Sink into my chair. Take my distance. No longer outside myself, standing at the frontier between land and sea like a roadside cross on which the wind and all my earlier life unfurl in salty waves. Let a thirty-five-year-old man pass in the distance, in his ecclesiastical garb and a two-day beard, his rifle over his shoulder. Am I to inhabit my youth once again like a garment picked off a chair? Let the voice of Felicity Jones be silent forever, scolding her son as if he were five years old.

"You're tracking that girl. You ought to shave and change your clothes."

In actual fact two men are on the lookout on the road this morning. He, in his big American car, drives slowly along the edge of the road, in a cloud of dust. I, with my rifle, walk along the shoulder of the road, half in the ditch. And she, the girl, hopping from foot to foot ahead of us, her red-brown hair disheveled, her green dress hiked up by the wind, revealing her knees as it clings to her thighs.

At the general store I shake the white dust from my feet and ask for Old Chum tobacco. Now she smiles, showing all her white teeth. Turns her head slightly toward me. Her somewhat hoarse voice asks for castille soap and nails. The man at the back of the store smokes, without taking the cigarette from his mouth, as if to hide his face in the smoke. He keeps looking at Nora behind his smoke screen. The general store smells of coal oil and tar . . . I have just enough time to warn Nora, tell her to be wary of strangers . . .

A moment later and I'll see her small laughing face raised up to me. Too late. The dark. No more pictures now. Once again, the solitude of the sleeping rectory and I, an old man, sitting stiff in his chair. The smell of coal oil and tar still lingers, spreads through the room like a blotch, filling my nostrils. Too uncomfortable to sleep in that chair. Cold on my back. My head drops onto my chest. Whether I sleep or not, rays of light pass before my eyes. Why not acknowledge at the outset that rustiness in the summer sun, that green stain moving with the russet rays along the beach. Time has shattered. Glitters now in scattered fragments, then is instantly tarnished in the hollow of my hand. If I look simultaneously out at the shore, the path that leads to the shore and the very top of the path, on the sandy road, I must be very careful to lose nothing of the scene, even if there is no way for me to know how it all began and just how it could have happened, one July morning in 1936.

The stranger stops his car at the side of the cliff, at the start of the path that goes down to the shore. He takes deep breaths of the sea air. His piercing eyes gaze at sea and shore like the black eye of the gannet aimed at the surface and depth of the water, spying through the waves on everything that trembles with life, that promises a feast.

I keep my eye on this man who is watching Nora, far away on the beach. I hate him in the way a minister of the Gospel—of all men—is not permitted to hate.

The stranger half-closes his eyes because of the sun; examines the pebble-strewn path that winds steeply down before him. Already the green spot haloed in red is moving along the path, ascending toward the stranger. Nora, on all fours, head down, concentrates on watching out for the pebbles that batter her ankles, her hands, her arms, ascends toward the road. A few steps from the stranger, making rapid progress toward him in a volley of pebbles and sand. If only she would raise her head, she could see the stranger's red socks, his pointed, highly polished shoes positioned at the very top of the hill, barring her way. He extends his hand to her. In just a moment she will look up, clasp the unknown, helping hand and . . .

Even today something in me insists on repeating that there is no holy wrath and that a man of God does not walk along the road with a rifle on his back. Too easy to shoulder it and fire two shots into the air to frighten the stranger and drive him away amid squealing tires and swirling sand.

The minister and his niece are face to face, in the dust from the road. The reddest heads in Griffin Creek (like foxes, Percival will say) look at each other at the side of the road. She laughs, all out of breath in the wind, her short hair blowing in her face. I slap her hard.

*The earth also was corrupt before God, and the earth was filled
with violence.*

Irene's broad face, a flat expanse of pale skin with a pug nose
and pinched lips. Why seek warmth and comfort from this
woman? It's as if my desire slips onto a stone. Irene pretends
to pray during the service, pretends to sleep at night when
I approach her, pretends to live as she always has, so it seems.
Beseech God to bless my marriage and grant me a son.

*Eye hath not seen, nor ear heard, neither have entered into the heart
of man, the things which God have prepared . . .*
Irene need only climb up the woodpile to reach the little
window in the boathouse. She could easily use her sleeve to
wipe the dust from the windowpane, clear away the dead
flies and cobwebs. Then she would see what Percival saw (his
moon face flattened against the glass). She would quickly
know just where she stands, better than Percival, she would
be clear in her own heart once and for all. But Irene never
walks on the beach. She's too busy inside the rectory. Taking
care of the minister's house. The minister's black suits. The
minister's white linen. The minister's pipes. She must be content with Percival's incoherent report. With his shouts. His
tears. Irene probably sent Percival away, back to his parents,
before he had a real fit on the carefully waxed floor of the
rectory. And then the sea is rough today, and it's a pleasure
for Percival to shout outside, amid all the commotion.
    Now she is once more assuming her dead woman's expres-
sion to greet the minister, her husband, as is proper, without
a hair out of place, without a shadow of a thought on her
smooth brow.
    My blazing head of hair above my face pale as a banner,
I lower my gaze beneath the ashen stare of Irene Jones, my
wife.
    Salt, pepper, butter, fresh pork, potato pancakes, rice pud-
ding, and black tea, each word enunciated, resounds in the
dining room, taking the place of conversation. When the last
sip of tea has been swallowed, Irene declares, without looking
at me, as if she were speaking to the wall,

"Everyone knows that the two most striking redheads in Griffin Creek look as much alike as father and daughter, though they're only uncle and niece."

A little later, lying in the dark, sensing at my side the regular breathing of Irene who sleeps close to the wall, I too give way to sleep and my sin gives way along with me, into the depths of night. It is as if I see my sin moving away through the little window in the boathouse, with the necessary distance, the detachment that is needed, while Percival howls at the window.

Nora straightens her dress, shakes off the sand and wisps of straw that cling to it, runs from me like the fury she has never ceased to be, while her little breasts were stiffening in my hands plunged deep in her bodice. I will probably never know the source of her fury that morning, though I took advantage of it like someone picking up crumbs under the table.

As for Percival's lies: *words, words, signifying nothing* . . . Irene has undoubtedly understood nothing.

Now she is curled even closer to the edge, until her bent knees strike against the wooden wall.

And base things of the world, and things which are despised, hath God chosen, yea, and things which are not, to bring to nothing things which are.

Lord, is it possible? Am I at this very moment to relive the summer of 1936, become once more a man who lusts after life and becomes a party to death?

The night of the barn dance Nicholas Jones dances with the Atkins girls, makes each in turn spin and whirl, holds them by the hand and waist, takes deep breaths of their odor, drunk without a single drop of alcohol, he moves rhythmically, forgetting his weight and the gravity of his responsibility.

Irene is there in her beige dress, bought from the catalogue. She refuses to dance, but sits beside the fiddlers, seeming not to hear them. Motionless, knees tight together, hands flat on her new dress, her colorless eyes staring into space, well above the dancers' heads, she cranes her neck to look at something invisible, very high up on the opposite wall.

The double door is wide open to the black countryside, shining brightly with stars and swirling with insects. The scent of new hay in the hayloft catches at our throats. The men take turns going out for a drink and a piss.

Stevens has kept his hat on his head, which doesn't prevent him from swinging lustily. His long legs move in rhythm, as if electrified, diabolical, furious.

Irene is like someone who looks across the street without seeing what's going on, the leaping and bounding in the very middle of the street that overflows with life. Yet she need only lower her gaze just a bit, to the level of the dancers' heads, to recognize the red hair of the minister, her husband. A glance to the side would enable her to see the table—a long plank set upon wooden trestles—the piles of sandwiches and cakes, the tin coffeepot full of hot coffee. At the same time, the image of her reverend husband, bowing to Olivia, to Nora, repeatedly kissing their hands, would hold no more secrets from Irene. Whereas Percival starts to cry in a gruff voice that is no longer that of a child.

But Irene's face remains chilly and impassive. Her gaze just now seems to see through the plank wall, very far into the countryside. I hear my mother Felicity consoling Percival, telling him the minister is not an ogre who devours girls' hands, but a poor man tempted by the devil.

But then shall I know even as also I am known. All will be clear in the light of Judgment. Beyond this world I shall see all Griffin Creek, from top to bottom, from side to side, as a land inhabited by men and women with living souls. And I shall see God face to face, and my sin will be as a shadow on my face. Only God will be able to wash away the shadow of my sin and all Griffin Creek with me, which I carry along in the shadow of my sin. Let no one escape. The village is surrounded. Stevens is with us for all eternity, not just passing through for a single summer, reduced to the terrible act of a single summer, one out of all the suns and moons that make up the summers of Griffin Creek. We are together, united, one to the other, for better, for worse, until the face of the world has gone by.

Summer 1936 the twins have scrawled right around the baseboard in the portrait gallery. Nora, Olivia, Irene appear endlessly, called by their names written in black poster paint on the wall of the gallery. They escape through the little corridor between kitchen and parlor. Insist on coming to keep me company during the too-long evenings. Daubed with paint following the wishes of the twins, rendered unrecognizable, yet resembling themselves, now all three of them sit on straw-bottomed chairs opposite me.

There is something surprising about Irene's steadfastness. A slight phantom since her birth, what then is the source of the tenacious image that passes my eyes now when I am old and stiff, sitting in my armchair?

Irene's discretion has always been remarkable. Never one word louder than the others. Neither fuss nor quarreling. Now she is effacing herself, like a drawing under an art gum. Without leaving a word of explanation on the kitchen table, she went and hanged herself in the barn. The little stool for milking the cow. The new rope she bought for the purpose at the general store. The woman knew what she was doing, why she was doing it, and she did it alone, at night, in the barn filled with new hay. Her husband the minister did not turn over in his sleep, did not notice the empty space in the big bed. It was only at dawn that he discovered her and held her in his arms one last time, cautiously, like someone carrying a long, dismembered statue.

No, no, I do not know that man or that woman. The scene has been shifted in time, a fragment of another life that was lost, ended with my dead youth.

Switch off the lights. Turn loose the viscous night, all through the house. Let it fill my eyes and ears. Until I no longer see. No longer hear. The past that throbs at my temples. Let the dead bury the dead.

Now that Irene is gone the Atkins girls are taking root in

their chairs, motionless and contemplative. I give them a long sermon until their bare legs swing, until their hands on their laps twine and untwine with fatigue. But in vain do I offer up as an example the strong woman of the Gospel, set Nora and Olivia on guard against the seducer clad in sheepskin, speak of him who comes like a thief, a wolf in the sheepfold, of the passing stranger who . . . Endlessly I ask myself which I prefer, Nora or Olivia, the one who is bronzed by the sun or the other who is golden as honey.

Percival's voice whistling in my ears. The child is mad. He had to be put away in Baie Saint-Paul. Why does his piercing voice still persist in my head, in spite of the time that has passed? Here he is declaring through his tears that his uncle Nicholas was there on the shore, near the boathouse, on the evening of August 31, and that the white moon made white spots, like lime scattered on the ground in the night.

Impossible to unlace my shoes. I lie on my bed fully clothed, pull up the covers as well as I can. The dark in the bedroom becomes gradually pale, turns gray. Through the dormer window comes a gray ever lighter and paler. Outside, the sun trails behind great ragged clouds. Somewhere in the countryside a rooster shouts himself hoarse, calling in vain for daybreak. Nothing moves yet in the sky, only an indistinct glow behind the dense clouds. One might think that day will never come. If we did not know from a reliable source, from having lived, that as long as the earth will turn, day will follow night and night will follow day. One day, however, it will be the end of the world. The accumulated gloom will no longer give way to the sun. The angel's flash will appear on the horizon. His metallic wings. His long silver trumpet. And the angel will proclaim in a loud voice that time no longer exists. And I, Nicholas Jones, minister of the Gospel in Griffin Creek, I shall be known as I am known by God.

It is only the rain. The first drops slow, heavy, widely spaced, slap against the shingles like bare footsteps. If day comes, it must appear through masses of gray cotton. Wait to awaken the twins. Now the rain pounds against the windowpanes, seeps under the flashing around the dormer window, drips onto the bedroom floor, soon it will reach the red woolen blanket on my bed and trace upon it spots even darker and redder than blood.

Bound into my old black jacket, the weight of shoes on my feet, I must have slept, the blanket pulled up to my chin. Saw in my dreams Percival, angel of the apocalypse, standing on the horizon, a man's body, a cherub's head, his cheeks distended from blowing into the Last Trumpet. Small black figures moving about on the beach, victims of desolation, listening to the voice of their despair, that thunders on the line between sea and sky. Finally they cover their ears with their hands.

For three days and nights Percival shouted at the top of his lungs. Starting when the Atkins girls disappeared, starting with the first searches on the beach, on the night of August 31, 1936. Percival began to howl like someone who knows where he stands and finds himself already face to face with the intolerable.

If day appears, it will be through masses of gray cotton. The day will be pale, like an endless dawn. Yet the Reverend Nicholas Jones must officiate at services today. This Sunday in October 1982 must have its hour of prayer and hymns so that the few survivors of Griffin Creek may come together in the little wooden church, faithful to the faith of the Lord, through time and dispersal.

All those who have left the village over the years have done so as if they gradually discovered that the land was too poor to be cultivated, the wind too violent to be borne, the hunting and fishing just good enough for vacations. But in reality, each of them wanted to become a stranger to the other, to escape the kinship that bound him to the people of Griffin Creek, guardians of the secret they must forget if they are to live.

Here they are at last standing in the doorway, wearing white

aprons and felt slippers: the twins bring me breakfast. The
day begins with fog and rain. They bid me good morning,
but nothing stirs on their intent little faces. Careful not to
vex me, they serve me black tea and buttered toast. Pat pre-
pares lather and shaving brush, fills the small blue bowl with
hot water. The rain lashes against the windows, runs onto
the bedroom floor. Pam has put a basin there. The sound of
drops of water, first ringing, then thudding. If the twins
rejoice at the rhythmical sound of the rain drumming into
the basin, feel an urge to clap their hands and dance around
it, they don't let it show. They unlace my shoes and bring
me clean socks.

In the time it takes an old man to dress from head to toe,
with no help from anyone, puffing like an ox, shouting for
his clerical collar, freshly bleached and starched, the shrill
bell of the church starts to ring through the fog. Some shut-
up houses are opened partway, along the savage coast, opening the way to creatures who walk unsteadily, heads down,
soaking wet under rain squalls. They could be counted on
the fingers of two hands. Joneses, Browns, Atkinses, Macdonalds, struggling survivors of the calamity of Griffin Creek.
They have wrapped their Bibles in plastic bags and now their
backs are bent under the rain as they head for the church
of their childhood, once white, now gray, under masses of
gray water.

Now Nicholas Jones, responsible for the word of God in
this land, pushed and pulled by the twins, heads in turn for
the church.

So that there is no rupture from God to them, my brethren,
because of me, their unworthy brother and legitimate priest,
I shall speak to them of God as I did in the past when the
world was innocent.

In the beginning there was only this taiga between Cap Sec
and Cap Sauvagine, and they came here, men, women, children, trailing after them quantities of objects, furniture and
clothing of all sorts, coming from New England. And the
Word was made flesh and dwelt among them.

The voice of Nicholas Jones not velvet now, but broken
and breathless, it hammers against the wooden walls. Old

faces look up at the minister, frowning somewhat as they struggle to pay attention.

Honor thy father and thy mother, says the minister, addressing the old people of Griffin Creek, *that thy days may be long upon the land which the Lord thy God giveth thee.* Amen.

LETTERS FROM STEVENS BROWN TO MICHAEL HOTCHKISS

Summer 1936

Make us tremble with thy desire, crude sea.

Pierre Jean Jouve

June 20, 1936

DEAR OLD MICK,

Well, I've traveled North America from Key West to the Laurentian Mountains, and now I'm back on home turf. When a man wants to go somewhere, any means of transportation is fine. I've tried them all: the train, the Greyhound bus, trucks, and other people's cars, when they were kind enough to pick me up, which wasn't very often. Because of my beard. Funny how a two- or three-day beard makes such a bad impression on those clean-shaven fellows from Georgia or the Carolinas. Only niggers make such a bad impression, as they stand by the roadside in the full sun wearing their faded clothes, still as statues, alone or in small family groups, waiting for a lift the way others might hope for heaven. Since I left I've been sticking close to all the indentations along the Atlantic coast, following the habit I've had since childhood of always being near the sea, its broad and salty breath, the creaking flight of gulls. I seldom lose sight of the coast, only every now and then if the roads or the railways go inland. But I always come back to the sea. During this journey I've spent some time working with niggers in the cotton fields, but I've also spent whole days breathing the wind from the sea, on the shore, bent over the gutting tables. With a good sharp knife I'd rip the insides out of little fish that shimmered in the sun and slithered in my hands. A cloud of wild birds would wheel around my head, clamoring stridently, and I'd have to chase them away like flies. By nighttime I reeked so, the women had no choice but to leave me in peace. Working with fish is like taking holy orders: it protects you.

I often think about our bungalow sitting there on the finest, whitest sand in the world, made of crushed shells there on the shore of the Gulf of Mexico where the water's transparent—turquoise in the sun, with violet patches when the clouds cast their shadows. I remember those tiny shellfish the waves would wash up at dusk, that we had to snatch up very fast before they disappeared in the sand. We'd make exquisite soups from them. The sand was so fine, shimmering pink and mauve, that sometimes if I awakened at night and looked out the window, I'd think I was seeing freshly fallen snow. Countryside as flat as your hand, a flat cake made of white sand, a few stunted trees, a few cows and horses, scrawny inedible hens, metered water that cost dear, the tiniest lawn worth a small fortune because of the shortage of water—only orange groves as far as the eye could see . . .

And that's where I met you, old buddy, and I didn't much like you at first glance, with your nasal singsong voice, the way you laughed when you talked and dropped your *r*'s which made all your unfinished sentences incomprehensible. You were always laughing and your face was all creased from laughing, and on those rare occasions when your face was still for a moment, there were little white lines all over your sun-tanned cheeks, especially around the eyes. Your laughter had woven a web of pearly scars, protected from the sun.

You'll say I write an odd sort of letter, that I ought to be telling you about the country around here, and the people, instead of describing your average American face and the sizzling state of Florida that you know better than anyone, since you were born there and live there still, in a tumbledown bungalow with bashed-in window screens, at 136 Gulfview Boulevard, facing the sea. Far in the distance, the horizon: the gaze grows weary looking for it, there's nothing to light on, it gets lost along the way, on the surface of the water, it founders in dream before it's even traveled across the vast space. Here the same escape is offered by the outstretched sea, here too, as far as the eye can see, the gaze is arrested by revery. Certain ecstasy. But the shore holds us longer with its rocks, red, brown, or gray, its austere mountains that are called dreary, like unpleasant people, its thickset fir trees, one in five dried-up and red, the dead not gathered but held tight by the living, upright, dried-up, and red among the living, green and black, wild vegetable life, breathing vigorously against the dead, holding them up among the living, unable to be rid of them, lacking the time, too busy, too powerfully occupied with life, with growing in size and multiplying in this impoverished soil where living is a challenge and a victory.

At first when I came to Griffin Creek, I thought the land and sea were drained of color. Their muted tones glowed dully, even in full sun. The sea seemed drab, only faintly green in fine weather, breathing like an animal lying on its back, wild with life, perturbed by the vast ebb and flow of its blood. You'll understand: I had such vivid memories of the dazzling colors of the landscape around Gulfview Boulevard, its brightly colored flatness, the very substance of the water sustained color as dazzling as the spreading sun, to taste the life which in these parts is secret, withheld, and begins to vibrate only when the eyes are free of any foreign body. I had to return here with the brand-new gaze of childhood, not yet clad in brilliant images, so as to grasp the savage beauty of the land that gave me birth.

June 30

After five years' absence I'm back in the fold. I'm sitting by the edge of a stream that bears my name: Brown Stream. It's written in black, in tar, on a board nailed to a post. I enjoyed seeing my name at the entrance to the village, to let me know I'd really come home, after all my peregrinations in foreign lands. Sitting on my rock at the edge of the bubbling, limpid stream, I've measured the time that's gone by since I left. I've measured my man's body, from head to feet, and inside myself I felt something dark, something powerful and undeniable: the intact presence of my body as a child, with its joys, its sorrows and fears. I was like a pregnant woman at the side of a road, catching her breath after a long walk, a woman heavy with her fruit. I looked for a long time at the village before deciding to walk down to it. I was at the top of the sandy hill, and the village was at the bottom, between the sea and the mountain, its white, precarious houses set awry to thwart the nor'easter. For reassurance, I told myself that the blood in my veins was no longer the same, nor was my skin, both having been renewed throughout my body, several times, since my departure. But it was only by thinking of my boots and hat that all my self-confidence and assurance were restored. I told myself that a man has nothing to fear if he's shod in manly boots, summer and winter, his hat screwed onto his head where it stays, even in church, even before women. I could have taken those houses I saw in the distance from the hilltop, held them in my hands and turned them over and over, made small figures emerge from them and hold them, too, between thumb and forefinger. But they probably contain too much that is new now, too many changes, births and deaths, the signs of passing time. Has my mother's face withered, do my father's fits of rage still keep him warm, prevent him from succumbing completely to boredom and contempt? For a moment the mad and comforting notion of going and throwing myself at the feet of my grandmother, Felicity, and asking for her blessing and her absolution. Her old hand on my forehead, ruffling my hair. For her alone I would take off my hat, I would kiss the hem of her dress. Above all, don't start with my parents' house: postpone the greeting, the confrontation, with the authors of my days. Stroll around for a while, hesitate among the houses, carefully select my door and front steps before setting foot inside, anywhere. The trouble with this village is that you need only cross a threshold, thinking you're alone, when all at once, from the neighboring windows, on all the doorsteps, sharp eyes suddenly appear like so many little claws, to clutch you and take hold of you.

My grandparents' house is the last one, at the very end, with a green fence and a wooden windbreak, not far from where they dry the herrings. I shall go look for my grandmother, hat in hand; I'll kneel on the ground before her and say: "It's Stevens, your grandson. I've come back and I salute you." Perhaps she won't recognize me. And what if no one in the village recognizes me? Then I'll simply retrace my steps, like someone who realizes that the road before him is closed off, like a horse that stumbles on some insurmountable obstacle. With my pack on my back, I'll take to the road again and travel the length and breadth of North America, living off jobs and off the seasons themselves, which are different from one province, from one state, to another. A whole continent in which to live and die in ease, almost the whole world to breathe in through my nose, my mouth, through all the pores of my skin, like an ocean to dive into and grow more and more agitated and alive, like a fish in water.

From the top of the hill I gaze down at the village. Arms folded under my head, stretched out full length on my flat rock at the edge of the stream, I raise my leg, blink, move my foot, shod in its dusty boot, over the village, hiding it completely. My foot is huge, and the village under it is very small. So small I can never return there, with my big boots, my man's stature. It must be stifling there. I place my foot over the village and make it disappear, then uncover it again, in all its smallness and fragility. I play at possessing the village and losing it, at will. All that because I can't make up my mind to walk down that hill and knock on one of the doors of this tiny sleeping village. And yet, I need only knock and immediately the door would be opened; I need only say, "It's me, Stevens, I'm back . . ."

And now a silhouette that seems to have been cut out of black or brown paper has just loomed out from behind my grandparents' green fence. The shadow moves with difficulty, on awkward legs. I think it's my grandfather, heavy and tottering now with age. He heads for the drying shed, examines the herrings that gleam like gilded bronze in the sun, he turns them over, imbibing their stench, then he comes and sits under a fir tree behind the green fence, in the little garden. If I shut one eye and put my foot over the houses at the bottom of the sandy hill again, I can make my grandfather disappear as he dozes with his back against the tree. Under the boot I picture the daily life of the old man, who must be seventy now. I could crush him like a cockroach. But I leave him there to sleep and dream under my sole, his dreams ascend the length of my leg like so many diligent ants, then burst in my head like bubbles. I know what my grandfather's thinking, as well as if I'd drunk from his glass. He presses against the fir tree, the resin that's been warmed all day, that scents and seeps into his clothes, his skin, his backbone. He adheres perfectly to the rough trunk. The notion of tree is so strong in his mind that my grandfather becomes the tree, with its mother branches, master branches, glutton branches, its infinite twigs and branchlets. So many offshoots for just one man, legitimate and not, enough to stay green and never die. The children, grandchildren, and even the great-grandchildren, ever since Isabel . . . Blessed, all that is blessed. My grandfather becomes confused, counts the households in the village, as if he were taking a census of a myriad of blue eyes that have sprung from a living source in the middle of his man's belly. Though he moans and tells himself he's old now, too old and too fat, with a big belly and no more seed, his posterity is there before him, spreading out even beyond the village, covering the hill like the sand on the beaches here, gray and granular, and it's useless to try and count them.

I have the power to make my grandfather exist, at the tip of my foot, or to abandon him to opaque sleep and silence. I opt for the latter solution. I'm tired of living by proxy. My real problem is knowing at which end of the village to start, without awakening the pack, without having them on my tail, my parents in the lead, avid and curious. Bombarded with questions, I'll be bombarded with questions like Lazarus leaving his grave, and like Lazarus I won't know how to answer, for real life is like death, impenetrable and profound.

If I decide on Maureen Macdonald, née Brown, it's because my cousin Jack's widow has a tiny little house hidden under the trees, way down at the bottom, and because it's the first house on the right when you come down the sandy hill. So I'll start with Maureen.

July 1

The woman was expecting me. I tell you, Mick, she was expecting me. That's likely why I was attracted by her house, out of all the others. She's middle-aged, a widow on top of all that, filled with all the expectations of a woman and a widow who gets up in the morning and wonders how she'll spend her day. She was wearing a man's jacket over her nightgown. She flung the kitchen door wide open, then stood there on the threshold, breathing deeply as if she were doing her exercises. From my hiding place behind the woodpile I could see her woman's bosom rise and fall inside her man's jacket. The smell of the sea must have pleased her, for she went on breathing deeply, calmly, without flagging, absorbing iodine and wrack as if her only reason for existence were to take deep breaths and to be present at the morning, there on her threshold at the seaside.

The land gleams with liquid light, earth, sky, and water radiant as far as the eye can see. Two rickety little apple trees are in blossom on either side of the door, a pink and white mist just barely attached drifts above the trunks and twisted branches. The activity in Maureen's kitchen is clean and precise, almost joyous, as she shifts saucepans, throws logs on the fire, slams the door of the cast-iron stove. Soon the bacon is sizzling in the pan, the coffee is starting to smell good, fragrant cooking odors drift through the screen door, driving away the great exhalations of the sea that are so compelling in the morning.

"Hello, Maureen Macdonald, née Brown. Your house smells good this morning."

With my nose pressed against the screen door, I must look like a flattened ape. Through the little holes in the screen I sniff intently my cousin Maureen's breakfast. Hunger tugs at my stomach. She leaves the stove, turns on her heel like a pivot, looks at me with eyes like pale stones in a face of darker stone, holding her knife and fork like weapons.

"It's me. Stevens. Don't you recognize me?"

A hoarse cry escapes from my cousin's throat, soon words

are tangled in her mouth, and I hear a voice from my child-hood that I thought I'd never hear again.

"Stevens! Sweet Jesus! I don't believe it! Look at you, you've shot up like a weed. Come in, lad, let's have a good look at you."

Once the hugging and kissing are over, I sit at the table and immediately eat two eggs with bacon, prepared by Maureen, who is drooling with pleasure, then I ask for two more.

Maureen breaks the eggs on the edge of the pan. Her gestures are precise and calm. I think she's happy to be feeding a man, to be given orders by him. I'm not being conceited now: I can feel it in every one of her gestures, in the very manner of her gestures—a contentment, a happy satisfaction.

I drink another strong scalding coffee. The bacon writhes in the pan, the eggs cook, I like them shiny, not too firm or too liquid, but just right. I give in to Maureen's know-how, to her powerful, somewhat rough hands. I wolf down my second helping of bacon and eggs without looking up from my plate, only Maureen's hands are still visible, as if detached from her body, fluttering above the table right under my nose. Now a stack of buttered bread and blackberry jam is placed before me by Maureen's hands. Then nothing. Nothing more. There is nothing more on this table that is edible, not a single crumb or drop, only Maureen's hands . . . I believe I'm satisfied. I lick my lips. Look up at Maureen, who has had her eye on me for a while now, hands at her hips. It's as if this woman, who hasn't eaten a thing since the night before and has given me her own breakfast, is satisfied merely by watching me eat, sharing my greed and my own satisfaction.

A sort of understanding, or rather a complicity between us. I forbid her to talk about my parents. She replies gently that I'm a bad, ungrateful son—smiling as she says it. I look at her, my chair tilted back, eyes half-shut in the smoke from my cigarette. A man's old jacket, a faded old nightgown, a face on the point of becoming completely hard, which certain actions by a man could hold off for a while, on the edge of the gulf. Her hair is magnificent, heavy, darker than the people around here, almost black, illuminated here and there by silver threads that gleam like hoarfrost. Now there's a sort of wildness in her gaze that's riveted to mine. I have a power. If I was able to bring my grandfather to life at my boot tip a while ago, now I sense a muffled cry in Maureen's bosom. Lord, is it possible, such brutal joy welling up in her, sharp as a knife? I don't look all that good with my three-day beard, my clothes and dirty boots covered with dust and dried mud. And yet the wild idea is making its way into Maureen's head. Later, she'll swear to me that at that very moment she wanted nothing so much as to wash me all over, like a grubby child. I offer her my services for the summer. I could be her hired man for the summer. She answers rabbits, hens, gardening, assures me there's plenty of work. But my cousin's voice is flat, toneless. She lets herself slip to my feet, limp as a rag doll. In a breath . . .

"First, off with your boots, then I'll heat up some water."

Maureen has prepared my bath in the big, blue-rimmed enameled tin washtub. She offers me her husband's razor and shaving brush. But she insists on washing me herself, pouring over me pitcher upon pitcher of water. In a moment I can see that she has no more strength at all in her arms and legs. She starts to tremble. I see a big vein throbbing in her neck. There's water spilled all over the kitchen.

Naked and streaming, I carry her into her room, onto her unmade bed. She protests, says she can't, her husband's been dead for ten years, she's no longer a woman or anything like one, she's too old . . .

So you see, dear Mick, I didn't drag my feet, I settled in right away, not all that easily as it happens, since my cousin Maureen was tight as a mouse hole, but I took root in the belly of a woman, and all around me the countryside of my childhood murmured like the sea.

July 5

I've become my cousin Maureen's hired hand. I weed her lettuce and cabbage, I feed, slaughter, and skin her rabbits, I re-cover the roof of the shed with new shingles, well soaked in creosote, Maureen's hard nipples are the color of peach pits, from time to time I give her a tumble during the day, between two jobs, in the kitchen, behind the rabbit hutch, my urge diminishes as she awakens under me, like a cat in heat. At night, despite her protests, I sleep in the barn, the model servant, I tell her over and over it's my appointed place and that I'd only make it hot in the bed, that her long hair tickles my face, to say nothing of her arms around my neck and her head on my chest. I ache all over. I intend to sleep alone at night and to satisfy myself, alone, if the urge takes me. Let my cousin Maureen discover at leisure, as she lies in her marriage bed, a new solitude greater than her first.

The hay in the barn is as dry as dust. You can tell that Maureen's husband has been gone a long time. Mower and hayrake rust in the dark. I can hear rats squealing. The night, like dark water, enters between badly joined planks, the buzzing of insects passes over my face, I sink into the old hay as if it were a mattress. I dream of returning to Florida, of buying a truck and selling oranges by the bushel from door to door. The two of us could join forces, old Mick, we'd make a killing. But in the meantime I'll call on the family and take up my life where I left off five years ago, after a fury worse than most. I've told you about it a hundred times at least, during those long winter nights on Gulfview Boulevard, both of us sitting on the porch with all the lights out, our cigarettes glowing red in the dark, the beach at our feet white as snow. The heady aroma of orange trees spreading out in vast waves. The sea close by.

July 8

I walk along the shore of Griffin Creek. Silvery driftwood, slippery seaweed with swollen seeds that I burst as I walk on them. The few shells are thick and gray, for the little creatures inside need a sturdy, waterproof house to protect them from the cold. (Remember those delicate pearly shells, the luminous beach, the transparent water, do you remember them, old buddy?) Today I go walking in icy water, on sand as sodden as baker's dough. The frosty vise tightens about my ankles. And those two tall teenaged grasshoppers in their woolen swimsuits were romping in it the other morning, along with my grandmother, crying out with delight. I don't recognize these creatures, half-woman, half-child (that supremely perverse intermediate age), amid the brood of kids from my own childhood, in the great confusion of boy and girl cousins that clutter my memory. Percival maintains that my grandmother is a dolphin with only one desire—to carry her two granddaughters out to sea on foaming steeds. From there it's a short step to bestowing on them sardines' tails, nimble fins, and brains the size of a raspberry seed. There's no holding back my brother Percival's imagination, the crazy things he dreams up, nothing to keep him from toppling over the edge into extravagant behavior and tears. With him, everything ends in tears and cries. It's probably too many constraints and prohibitions that have brought him to this tearful state. A man's body, a child's mind, desire and fear—it's all unreconcilable, and Percival feels sorry for himself. He, at least, I recognized immediately the other morning, amid the rushes, eyeing his cousins as they swam, and drooling with despair. Overly round blue eyes in a baby's face, a heavy noggin that droops toward his shoulder. All that's unchanged since I went away, except that now his childlike head sits atop an exceptionally large and robust body. A sort of giant with a cherub's face. Percival is fifteen, Maureen told me. With his woolly head in my hand, he rubs against me like a curly little dog. My brother is an idiot.

It's understood that I'll go and see them all, one after another, ending with my parents, so public rumor can prepare them properly for my visit and put them in the state of exasperation necessary if they're to greet me as usual.

It didn't take long. I said to Percival, "Hello, I'm your brother Stevens," and he told everybody right away, his strange gait, rhythmic and heavy, going from house to house, like a conscientious peddler.

I start with the children. It's not hard to recognize most of them, at once. Maureen decided to take me with her to pick strawberries. They're already there, squatting in their bright clothes all down the field, along the rim of the forest.

Heads are raised, eyes peer out from under straw or linen hats. I'm seen, examined, weighed, judged, my heart's in my boots. I in turn squat, while the childlike glances turn away from me, back to the strawberries hidden under the leaves.

The sun beats down on napes and bent shoulders. The sweet perfume of the strawberries, the red warmth of the earth close to us as we breathe it. Our fingers stained red. It's no job for a man, and I stand out among the women and children. The strange sensation that suddenly a small animal is pressed against me, and I can feel its heartbeats and light breathing. One of the children has silently approached me in the trampled grass. A girl. Her bare arm against my shoulder, her warm earthy odor. Now she turns her head toward me. Her linen hat tipped back. Her eyes screwed up, the color of the sea, her dazzling smile, her little pointed face flecked with freckles, like a sparrow's egg. She tells me that her name is Nora, that she's my first cousin. Percival has already told her I'm here.

The stroke of noon. The shade that we've longed for since morning. The water we drink from the tin pail is warm. The bread is soft, the ham melting in the sun. My cousin Nora examines me suspiciously, sitting firmly with her knees to her chin, arms around her knees, her head on her arms. A little animal, I tell you, a glossy little animal lying in wait in the grass.

Good old Maureen makes kettles full of strawberry jam that fills the whole house with its fragrance. I skim the boiling pink foam as it forms, floating on the dark, gleaming syrup. Carefully I spread it on bread and eat it straightaway.

July 12

A mere nothing fulfills me. I like long summer days that last until late in the evening. Maureen's house, Maureen's garden, Maureen's outbuildings have never looked better. The woman can't get over having close to hand, combined in a single man, a servant and such a demanding master.

I'm being tracked. No matter what I do someone spots me

coming or going, I'm spied on, recognized. When I pass, people greet me—or sometimes turn their heads. Invisible hands lift curtains from windows, hidden eyes observe me behind rocks on the beach. My parents already know. They must be expecting me, sitting out on the gallery, all dressed up and rocking in their rocking chairs, one red, the other green, both with seats of woven straw.

The children have been following me, step by step, since I started playing my mouth organ. I order them to form a line behind me, and we march across the village in procession to a tune on the harmonica. I dream of emptying Griffin Creek of all its children and taking them away with me, beyond the horizon. Like that piper who . . .

The little girls go to great pains to please me. They cling to me like spruce gum. Nora wanted to learn to play the mouth organ. She likes putting her lips on the harmonica as fast as possible after I've stopped playing. I can taste you, cousin Stevens, your music, your saliva, and your lips, and you'll taste me too, you'll taste Nora Atkins, your cousin. She blows her little tune and offers me the instrument, all wet.

"Taste it, it's as if we were kissing."

She laughs, her hair in her eyes, an auburn stain in the light.

July 15

No use looking for extraordinary reasons. If I came back, it was simply to look around. Out of curiosity, I tell you. For lack of anything better to do. Out of nostalgia too, most likely. I saw my grandmother again, and she kissed me and offered me plum cake and tea. As soon as she saw me in the front door, she gave a sort of cry filled with tender, savage words all tangled up together.

"Stevens! My little boy, my big boy, so tall, my grandson, better looking than his father, so tall, smarter than his mother, sharp as a tack with a heart as hard as a rock, Aunt Agnes's eyes, his grandfather's nose, hair like mine, his grandmother's, when I was young, on the boy's head, a mass of blond hair on his hard head . . . Stevens, dear Stevens."

She examined each one of my features. A portrait under a magnifying glass. A deep sigh. My grandmother's excitement drops, is slowly absorbed in that sigh, like a strong wind grown suddenly calm after exhausting its force and momentum. Very softly now, clenching her teeth, she declares that I'm just like my grandfather, can't be trusted, and that all men are pigs.

My grandmother's tea is black as ink, acrid on the tongue long after you've swallowed it. She talks to me about my cousins Nora and Olivia. I find out that three jealous men keep Olivia inside a big house with a carved wooden gallery all around it. Since her mother's death, she's never been less free, though she's seventeen now, with a father and two brothers to feed, to wash and iron and mend for, her dying mother having made her promise to take good care of all three of them, and to obey them absolutely.

My grandmother advises me to wipe my feet carefully the next time I come to see her.

My grandmother has always preferred girls.

July 19

Three in the afternoon. The sea shimmers like tin in the sun, dazzling us. A sort of torpor numbs the countryside. The wind sleeps in the sun, awakens at times with a muffled rumbling, then sleeps once more, stretched out upon the fields and sea. The cries of birds that sound slaked and sated start up again here and there, without much conviction.

For a while now I've been looking at Olivia's house as if it were transparent, I've been imagining Olivia's life inside it, making her ascend and descend the stairs at will, I see her putting on her stockings and sewing, utterly occupied for long hours, her calm arm and hand endlessly drawing the needle and thread.

I am planted there like a fence post, in front of Olivia's house, in the bright blinding sun. I know that one of her brothers, the one with the coast guard, is asleep upstairs, exhausted after a night of frantic pursuit on his boat. He must sleep like the dead. Only his beard's still alive, darkening his face.

Now the wind is blowing relentlessly. The fields are ridged by the wind into endless billows of hay and wild oats. I walk in the wind which muffles the sound of my footsteps. Now I am on the kitchen steps, against the screen door. Olivia is ironing a man's shirt, on a board supported by two chairs. Her precise, confident movements. Her short dress, faded blue. She hasn't noticed me yet, and it's as if the strange, slow wind were passing straight through her, deep into the most secret part of her life. Open to the four winds: the girl is open to the four winds, I just have to put in an appearance and . . . Twice she glances over her shoulder, like someone whose mind is not at rest. Like a bird at the top of a tree when a cat, hidden in the leaves below, shakes the whole trunk with claws that aren't yet visible.

The framework of the house creaks like the hull of a boat in a raging storm. The wind whistles under the doors of the shut-up rooms. Olivia is put increasingly on her guard by the wind. Someone walking on the gallery? Footsteps on the ground and in the grass around the house? Eyes at the windows? Someone moving in the attic. It's just my cousin Olivia's imagination at work, while I, appearing and disappearing behind the screen door, watch her and feel her, all warm and alive, just two steps away from me. Suddenly I am caught in the blue gaze of Olivia who stares at the door with a look of alarm. I'm accountable for my appearance, which is hardly reassuring, plastered against the screen. Tall and lanky, my hat shading my eyes, I call her by name.

"Hey, Olivia! Olivia Atkins! Hi, there!"

Her eyes filled with alarm, too wide, too blue, it seems to me. She calls me "Mister" and asks me what I want, without leaving her ironing board, as if it were a necessary barrier between us, though the door's still shut and I'm behind it, my face distorted by the screen. I laugh. My laughter passes through the little holes in the screen, shattering into a thousand slivers on the kitchen floor at Olivia's feet. She shrinks back as if a snake were struggling there at the tips of her shoes. In a barely audible voice she lets me know that her brother Patrick is upstairs.

"It's you I want to see, Olivia Atkins, not your brother. I'm your cousin Stevens."

Olivia seems not to understand. She stands there behind her ironing board, arms dangling, and you could even think she wasn't breathing.

"You won't let me in?"

Olivia turns harder and harder, turns to a stone statue behind her ironing board. I'm sure she must be thinking of her brother upstairs, of calling to him for help, with all the strength of her soul.

"You won't let me in?"

"Tell me what you want, right away. Don't bother coming in."

I laugh harder.

"Tell you what I want, just like that, standing in the door, in this wind? Are you crazy?"

"I'm in a hurry."

She goes back to her ironing, with rapid little motions, not even aware of what she's doing.

"I want to talk to you. Let me in."

The smell of scorched cloth, a wisp of smoke. Olivia has just burned a cuff.

"Leave me alone. I'm going to burn everything."

"Why won't you let me in? Because I look like a tramp?"

Olivia drops the white shirt she was holding.

Now she resolutely approaches the door. Most likely wanting an end to it, once and for all. She examines me closely as if she had a duty to look at me and see me clearly. Ever since I've been standing there, crushed against the screen. I stiffen beneath her gaze. It's strange to be able to watch her from so close, to be watched by her. If I only laugh once, just once more, my face may shatter under Olivia's violet gaze and I'll be lost. Now it's as if she can no longer close her eyes. I'm the first one to look away. The girl is too beautiful, and I should wring her neck right away, before . . . I stammer,

"I saw you the other morning, soaking wet, coming out of the water, with your long hair hanging down."

At that moment Patrick came downstairs, stretching his arms above his head. He asked me in. He made me drink some bootleg alcohol, while Olivia bent her astonishing face over her iron again.

Was a certain remark really uttered by Olivia when I passed close to her, amid the odor of hot linen, or did I imagine it, so much did I think I could distinguish that remark being uttered by her whole tense and frightened body.

"I knew who you were right away, cousin Stevens. I'd have picked you out of ten thousand. But you aren't good and you shouldn't have been allowed in."

Olivia ironed six white shirts. Patrick and I drained the bottle.

July 23

To be someone else. No longer be Stevens Brown, son of John Brown and Bea Jones. Perhaps it's not too late to turn over a new leaf altogether. Abandon my old self by the road-side, an old castoff tossed in the ditch, with a brand-new soul that molts in the sun, and go back to square one. Not allow the rest of what happened to me at Griffin Creek unfold till the end. Run away before . . . Such excitement through my whole body, an inexplicable rage. There are too many women in this village, too many woman in heat and perverse children who dog my footsteps. I visit the relatives, going from one to the next. Women. Always women. It's not old Maureen now, or little Nora. Olivia is tougher, more resistant in her fear of me, her fear of what might come to her from me, from my wild body, my evil heart. The girl is torn between her fear of me and her attraction to me. I have seen her in her transparent house, her dress ripped off, her heart stripped bare and struggling. You know my power for sensing other people, for living and putting myself in their place. But I swear, at this precise moment in my life what I want more than anything else in the world is to exhaust that power in one go and become, without looking back, a new man who packs his bags and disappears beyond the horizon. Olivia's wisdom. Her fear of me. Olivia's protectors. A vague rattling of chains whenever she moves. Everything attracts me and keeps me here. I measure my margin of freedom, like a woman who's sewn a seam too close to the edge of the cloth and sees it fraying between her fingers. Olivia's father. Olivia's brothers. Their pale eyes, their shaggy beards, their hunting rifles. And I facing them, all alone, deranged and joyful.

When I left Olivia's house, little Nora was waiting for me by the side of the road. Her frail and stubborn silhouette, firmly planted in the ground, in the whirling wind. The sound of the waves, their deafening billowing, as far as the eye can see. The sulphur-colored sky.

Without moving, without even looking at me, her shoes gray with sand, her hair tousled, she talks to me about her cousin Olivia. Hoping to see Nora aglow with rage on the road, I reply that her cousin Olivia is very beautiful. Nora doesn't turn a hair. She talks in an even little voice, without inflection, as if she were reciting a lesson.

"That depends on your taste. I don't think she's all that beautiful. There's something wrong with her right foot. One toe's attached to the other by a little piece of skin, like a duck. It's disgusting."

"Are you telling me that because you're jealous?"

"Me, jealous of Olivia! Are you trying to insult me?"

She seems to be taking root in the dust. Her white teeth, her cheeks red, as if she had a fever. With an abrupt thrust of her whole body, her mane blazing, Nora leaps onto the road. Runs away. Hurls at me as she runs words of rage that lose their edge in the space and the wind, with the slight sound of her running shoes.

"Cousin Stevens, I hate you!"

I laugh. All alone on the deserted road.

July 25

Believe me if you want, old Mick, but the thought of Olivia's webbed foot made me feel frustrated. Such a perfect crea-

ture—how could it be? I should have had her take off her
shoe and examined her foot, as you do to a horse. Who can
we trust if Beauty herself conceals a flaw in her shoe? The
girl is simply a hypocrite. No prettier or wiser than the others.
She looks as if butter wouldn't melt in her mouth. I'll unmask
them all. Draw out the only truth, from their pretentious
little backsides. Strip them of their cheap finery, reduce them
to mere desire, moist and hot, then stand them in a row, a
single bleating flock. Maureen, little Nora, Olivia too, most
likely. I have all the time in the world.

The story of a summer instead of real letters, because the
person they're addressed to never replies. Oh, you warned
me before I left. You hate writing. All the same, your silence
makes me feel uneasy about going on. I feel as if I'm writing
before a mirror which then reflects my scrawls reversed, un-
readable. I feel like burning all my letters before I mail them.
And yet, I must tell you the rest.

For the time being, I'm coming closer and closer to my
parents, all day I blow hot and cold when I think of them.
It's because of my young brother Percival, whom I'm tracking, rather as though by stepping in his footprints in the wet
sand I were rediscovering the marks of my own childhood.

Since last night the land has been shrouded in fog. We
hear foghorns here and there in the distance, that stir up
great emotions in Percival, who loves these strange sounds
that come from he knows not where. He claps his hands, and
his eyes are full of tears. You can see that the foghorns fill
him with delight and despair. In my own childhood I would
steep myself in fog and melancholy.

From time to time the thick white clouds will fray, revealing
the top of a mast that seems to slip past, alone, upon the sea,
separated from its decapitated boat, suspended in the fleecy
air.

All day, Percival plays at getting lost in the fog and I play
at getting lost along with him. Houses, barns, cows, horses,
milk churns go astray at will. But the most daring thing for
Percival is to try and lose his father and mother. Though he
runs on the beach, suspended in midair, till he's out of breath,
tasting the salty spray on his lips, letting the fog sweep over

him, swallowing it through all the pores of his skin, filling his eyes with it, and his nose, ears, and mouth, he never succeeds completely in escaping his parents' vigilance. Voices I know, words already heard, come to him, shot like arrows.

"Percy, here! Percy, there! Percy, it's time. Milking time. The milk pail. The churns. Percy! It's full to the brim, Percy. Pay attention! Be careful! And you mustn't run!"

The voices whistle around my head now, as in the past.

"Watch out! Watch out!"

He runs, joggling a pail full of milk that splatters his legs. He is covered with white mist, like a moving train, a galloping horse with steaming nostrils, at least he thinks so, and he runs, faster and faster. Soon he will be completely beyond his parents' reach, camouflaged by fog like a little octopus in its ink. In fact, he hasn't even passed the corner of the gray plank milk house, with its thick walls, double and triple, separated by sawdust.

Percival didn't see the slap coming and couldn't duck it. A drop of blood forms at the tip of his nose and drips onto his checkered shirt. Head buzzing, he gazes distractedly at the drop of blood on his shirt and at the big puddle of milk spilled on the sand at his feet. A tall stooped man I know well moves away giddily through the fog. A voice that hasn't changed bellows,

"You little bugger! Get out of here, goddammit! And don't show your face around here again!"

Sitting on the ground, leaning against the milk house, Percival struggles to keep still and to swallow the blood that drips down his throat.

My voice, very high above Percival, holding itself back from breaking. A sort of muffled softness that escapes me.

"I had my troubles too when I was younger."

My rough and awkward hand ruffles Percival's mop of hair. He raises his head and recognizes me standing there before him, legs apart, head lost in the mist, a small heap of unhappiness sitting on the ground, leaning against the gray plank wall.

"It's all right, you won't feel it on your wedding day."

To distract him, I show him a switchblade I have in a

leather case hanging from my belt. I tell him that in Florida I've used this knife to peel rattlesnakes, like bananas.

"How about coming with me, Percival? We'll go around the world together."

He shakes his head sadly, not looking at me, a faraway look in his wide-open eyes, waiting for tears that don't come.

Two little girls the identical size, with straw-colored braids the same thickness and length, have just come into view on either side of Percival, to surround and protect him.

My brother Percival is crying now, sobbing hard. My twin sisters, who I thought were still in the cradle, are yipping like a nest of hawk owls, wiping Percival's nose and drying his eyes with a kitchen rag.

July 28

The shadow of my parents draws closer and closer. At night when I fall asleep in Maureen's barn, I hear the great double shadow whispering behind the thin partition. Something about children already born that should be lost in the forest before they're too big. I'll tell Percival and the twins. I'll take them all away with me, in a bright red fire-engine with all its sirens screaming. Assembled thus, we'll travel right across America without interruption, from end to end, as far as the orange groves you know so well. Don't worry, Mick my friend, I'm only dreaming. You needn't fear an invasion by my family. The whole rotten bunch is unique and non-transportable.

To be somebody else: it's something I can't get out of my mind. To organize my memories, arrange images, quite simply split myself in two and still remain myself. To be able to witness the life that I've lived, without danger, without being obliged to reenter it and say: Here I am, it's me, Stevens Brown, son of John Brown and Beatrice Jones. A kind of game you can withdraw from at will.

No sense fooling myself. Memories reverberate throughout my body, a living rumor in waves of sound, vibrating to my very fingertips. Tonight a feeling of cold gradually spreads through me as I watch over the night between the slits in the barn and the great double shadow beyond the darkness. The chilly night offers no explanation. This cold comes from somewhere else, from the muddled depths of birth, from the first strokes of my mother's icy hands on my infant body.

She has very poor circulation, according to Dr. Hopkins. She gives off cold the way other people give off heat. It's surprising she can even bring live babies into the world, from such a glacial belly you'd expect only corpses . . . These two are certainly alive. Two at once is too many, she says. She weeps and declares that she doesn't want these two children. Keeps saying, "My twins," holding one on each arm. A shudder runs down her spine. She shakes her head.

"I can't, I can't, I can't."

I shut my eyes. What's to be done with the twins? Shall we drown them like kittens, throw them to the pigs perhaps, or lose them in the woods? I run out of the room. When I tiptoe back in, I realize nothing's been done yet. The twins are still there, taking turns clinging to my mother's breast. She is pale and filled with trepidation, overflowing with milk like a frozen mountain. The whole bedroom shows the effects of this source of cold settled on the big bed, with a pair of newborns crying themselves hoarse. And I in my corner turn to ice, like a snowman. I hear my own voice, a small vein still liquid inside the ice. And I and I and I . . . It's not raw milk that she gave me, my mother Beatrice, but hunger and thirst. Desire. I must scream as hard as my brother Percival until my father kicks me out of the cold bedroom.

And why take offence at this tall, thin, stooped man, with his straight shoulders and chest, for after all he's only a shadow? Only anger can, sometimes, make my father's shadow shine and roar. I attract lightning like a wet tree standing in the middle of a field. John Brown must have good reasons for hitting his son's head, his son's back, his son's buttocks so hard, at every opportunity. He does it conscientiously, as if he were extirpating from the child's body the very root of the evil power that's been set loose in the house since the very beginning of time.

Have I told you all this before, old buddy, on one of those long evenings on Gulfview Boulevard? Have I tried before to explain my mother and father to you? A vain and frantic attempt at filial understanding. Simplify my parents to the limit, make them crystal clear, wicked through strength, themselves submissive to strength.

August 2

The very brief space of a summer, whittled down at both ends by the frost. Less than three months to seed, grow, and harvest. Less than three months to become man and woman, to live and to die. I think of Nora and Olivia, who are virgins. Soon they'll be married off and knocked up. The soil is barren in these parts, but when it sets to it, it blazes, becomes ardent and violent, eager to fulfill itself before it's too late. These people are dirt poor, but they don't know it. Confronted with nothing but their day-to-day existence, they have no imagination, no grounds for comparison. The sea and the forest belong to them, they draw joy and sustenance from them, but they can't communicate their savage inner life.

I think about Nora and Olivia more and more while I'm staying here, soon the Atkins girls will escape me altogether, they'll swing very quickly to the other side of the world. Married, pregnant, the pretty skin of their pretty bellies distended, their pretty breasts full of milk, they'll be left to women's rancor, locked away in their closed houses. How I hate the muffled world of women, the demands they whisper among themselves, all day long, especially in the summer when most of the men are at sea or in the fields. There's no one but my uncle Nicholas to calm them down, make them listen to reason, in the name of God and the law of the church, which knows how to put women in their place.

A little while, and ye shall not see me: and again, a little while and ye shall see me. I can't help it—too much Bible reading during my childhood no doubt—if there's anyone in this village who resembles Christ that person is me, Stevens Brown. No so much because of the three-day beard and the hat pulled down over my eyes, but because I'm only passing through Griffin Creek. Just a little more now and I'll disappear as I came. I've made up my mind; September 1st I'll be on the road again, Florida bound. It'll take as long as it takes. I'm patient. Any means of transportation that's free is fine. I know I'll end up on some flat road, between two orange groves, as far as the eye can see, flat as the road with the hovering sun. And you'll be there too, old buddy, with your wrinkled smile, your hands full of oranges, and your friendship, if that's still all right with you. I'll be saved then, saved I tell you. But first I must go and say hello to my parents, then there'll be nothing left for me to do here. Time's running out. Already the fireweed's in bloom all along the ditches, through the fields. Their bright pink color sweeps over the countryside, in the light that is no longer altogether the light of summer.

August 6

The sun's vibrations cover a great area here because of the sea which reflects all the light in long swathes onto the fields, the big and little hillocks and, just a step away, the forest, vast preserve of game and odors. Red paths covered with pine needles. Paths spotted with yellow and powdered by larches with sad dull gold.

Needles and dead leaves creak under my cousin Nora's tread. She's following me at a distance in the woods, hiding here and there, behind trees, in the hollow of bushes. I don't turn my head, but I know she's there, very near, stubbornly following me, her desire for me keeping her there. Her stubbornness delights me. As I go along, my veins secrete a stubbornness that matches hers, as alert and weighty as hers.

I refuse her with as much vehemence as she desires me. A test of strength. It's always like that, I think, whenever a girl makes advances to me. They must toe the line, all of them. I've already started breaking in old Maureen. More and more, I deprive her. Tell her she's old, that I'll be leaving soon.

I turn around. Leaning against a tree, I watch little Nora arrive, in the shadow of the trees. She stops and looks at me with eyes like a hare surprised by a hunter. I talk to her, a little too shrill, a little too loud.

"What're you doing here? Why are you tracking me?"

I think she utters my name, "Stevens," so low that my name, hardly out of her mouth, already seems to belong to the multitude of confused sounds that exist in the forest. In another place, silence would already have fallen between us, like a knife, but silence is impossible here because of the living murmur all around. I don't budge. I watch her coming. I wait for her to decide. For a long moment she stands there, motionless, as if wavering, in her green dress and her scorched red hair. I think she says "Stevens" again, like a half-swallowed moan. Now she advances, taking short steps, in the dead leaves and scrub bushes. It would be easy to push her over onto a carpet of humus and merge with her into the strong odor of the earth, easy to do with her what no man has yet done with her, to deliver her from that first time, so important to girls, and enable her henceforth to welcome all the boys who want to, it would be easy to fornicate with her and send her home to her father and mother, my uncle and aunt, with a trickle of blood between her thighs.

I let her approach very close. I listen to her rapid breathing, I count her freckles, I admire the length of her eyelashes. Her gaze lowered, mouth swollen, her expectation perceptible all through her frail body, just two steps from me. I guess rather than read on her lips my name uttered for the third time, "Stevens." I believe, too, that she is begging me to kiss her. I do so straightaway, half-heartedly, on both cheeks, as if I'm weary, as if I must clearly establish the sort of relation that must exist between us. I speak to her as to a child entrusted to my care.

"Don't do anything you'll regret later."

She stiffens, freezes. For a moment she seems absent, protected by her impassive face, quite taken up, in the depths of her being, with receiving the insult, swallowing it like some bitter potion. Gradually her eyes brighten, the tears come slowly, drown her gaze, glide onto her cheeks. I rather enjoy that. But just now as I'm starting to really have fun I see her fury explode. Oh I like you this way, little cousin, in a fit of rage, and how I'd love to take you now, here in these deep woods. She calls me a "rotten son of a bitch" and a "bastard," she hunts for another word she doesn't know yet and calls me a sissy. Still, I don't try to keep her there on the path and she moves away, tripping over stumps and dead branches.

August 9

I've made up my mind, I'll go see my parents this very evening. Maureen lent me one of her late husband's suits, which she took out of mothballs. The pants and the sleeves of the jacket had to be let down. I shaved carefully and Maureen cut my hair with her big sewing scissors. Now there's a funny white mark on my neck between the hair and the tanned skin. In the mirror I can see the white line and the marks left in my hair by Maureen's gleaming scissors. She's lucky, because instead of getting mad I burst out laughing. But things go completely sour between us when I tell her I intend to keep my hat on all evening at my parents'. All dressed up as I am, in a man's suit and a man's hat, I have no intention of baring my head to my parents like a naked child who bows his head as he waits for his punishment. I tower over them now with my man's stature, in all my man's clothes, my man's hat and boots, and they must be aware of it. The visit I'm paying them tonight is an official one, in official costume, my official man's costume, somewhat like a serviceman with his gold buttons and his epaulettes, or a minister with his roman collar. The least you can say is that big shots like them don't take off their badges of office when they set foot inside their parents' house. Maureen's not convinced but, rather, incredulous and annoyed. I give her my last excuse just before I walk out the door, somewhat lightly, as if it weren't terribly important.

"Anyway, as far as my hat's concerned, I think it'll infuriate them."

Now I'm here with them in the little front room that's reserved for company. We're drinking beer. Trying to make conversation, sitting on uncomfortable little chairs, feet on the braided rug, hands flat on our knees. But time isn't passing, it drags on, heavy. It's as if an invisible presence were growing in the shadows, using up all the air around us, gradually preventing us from breathing. The final scene is there in the kitchen, just off to the side, spreading out and coming back to life. I'd just have to look through the open door to see the green and brown linoleum and the white lines indicating the exact positions of the characters at the moment when the scene is taking place. That's what policemen do after a tragedy in order to demarcate the location of the bodies on the ground. As far as my mother, Beatrice, is concerned, she's easy to recognize because she's standing, there's only the mark of her shoes on the floor. The other two bodies are on the ground, tangled and confused, transfixed there in mid-struggle, in their gestures of struggling and hatred. Grunts, cries, and groans petrified at the moment of their eructation persist in an eternal silent grimace.

We sip our drinks. Not one word is possible between us now. The intrusive presence breathes behind the kitchen wall. Glasses clink, beer moves from glass to mouth, tongues click, all these sounds languish in the heavy air. A certain moment in the shared life of the three of us is there, frozen forever. Fury motionless as a pond.

The father has exercised his right to punish, and the son has defended himself. Neither victor nor vanquished. The two protagonists are of equal strength. The mother shouts herself hoarse, in vain, begging them not to fight, but they'll go on as long as their breath holds out. Without tending to my bumps and bruises, I took off while the going was good and traveled across America. It was a matter of moving fast before my father came back to his senses and brought down his curse.

And now, five years later, we're there, all three, sitting on our little chairs, stilted and well-behaved, while John Brown mutters the sentence he hadn't pronounced against his son, shifts it from one side of his mouth to the other, between his teeth, like a wad of tobacco.

Percival and the twins burst into the house with a shout, go into the kitchen, passing right through the heavy shadow that lies on the ground without seeing it, without even sensing it, passing through it like a transparent cloud, giving free rein to their delight at seeing me. All three give me a warm welcome. With Pam's arms around my neck, I spread out my riches, my treasures of goodness and affection, under my parents' nose.

John Brown gives me another drink. His hand shakes. I am twenty years old and I'm stronger.

August 14

The light changes from day to day, as it moves toward autumn. Certain moments in late summer, in this grim landscape, attain an incredible fullness, an insane precision. Each black fir tree, picked out by the light, its every branch and needle standing separate from its neighbors (themselves standing separate, picked out), rendered unique by the light that grasps each tree bodily, pressing and squeezing it, exalting it against the sky's harsh blue, while the blue of the sky sways over the sea in great blue swathes fringed in white. Above the sea, between sea and sky, taut as a canvas cover that stirs and hums, a multitude of birds, white, brown, and gray, their deafening cries.

Tufts of sea grass pierce the sand, toss in the wind, seized by relentless vortices. In the hollows of reddish rocks, stagnant puddles, olive green, forgotten by the tides. Percival bends over these puddles, unmoving, nearly petrified with concentration. From time to time, gesturing sharply with his big childlike hand, he grasps a tadpole. And I, Stevens Brown, I look at the sea as if I'd never seen it before. In that water flecked with foam, where every wave billows and crackles like a bullet, like a thousand bullets fired at once, a crackling wall that forms, rises, reaches its summit, then immediately subsides, foaming on the sand, dying on the sand, in a small thread of foam like spittle.

I watch my cousin Olivia, who is swimming. I didn't recognize her right away, I even took her for her brother Patrick, because swimming in this choppy water, making the necessary movements, taking the wave just as it's forming, letting the wave carry you along, then descending into its hollow and starting again as if you were part of the water's pulsation, her own heart in tune with the huge heart of the moving sea, is the result of a such a mastery of one's own body I wouldn't have thought her capable of it. Patrick, who likes being in charge, has probably given her swimming lessons.

Ever since she's been hiding behind her household chores, sequestered by three men who are quick to take offence, her magnificent body embarrassed by the simplest acts because she's afraid of being herself, beautiful and desirable, blameless and acknowledged in the summer light. What do I know of her? A few words exchanged now and then when we meet. Nothing, less than nothing.

"Hello Olivia."

"Hello Stevens."

"Nice morning."

"Sure is!"

Still the same skin, the same unsociable air. I don't belong to myself, she thinks. I belong to them, to my brothers, my father too. To God who is watching us. I swore to my dying mother . . . Olivia's arms flutter above the wild raspberry bushes. The red berries shimmering violet in Olivia's fingers. Olivia's bare arms hanging wet sheets on the clothesline, behind her father's house. The sheets clatter like sails in the wind. Wisps of Olivia's golden hair in the wind. Her white dress blows about her long bare legs. Her fear rises a notch when I approach and stare at her. Her heart beats faster, like a bird in the hollow of a closed fist. So many images of her stored up in the course of the summer. Most of all, her delectable fear. The musky odor of her fear.

And now, this morning, the girl is free in the sea, as if I, with my evil heart, didn't exist, not I or anyone else. Alone in the world, in the water that gave her birth.

She sits on a rock, head bent forward, her hair brushed forward and sweeping her face. She doesn't hear me coming, my footsteps mingling with the water's roar. I try to take her in my arms: ice-cold and streaming wet, all out of breath, she struggles like a freshly caught fish, her long wet hair lashing my face. I whisper peculiar and flirtatious remarks having to do with a siren with webbed feet, exposed by Nora. I ask to see my cousin Olivia's duck feet.

Patrick, the master swimmer, or Sidney, I don't really know which of Olivia's brothers, this one or that, it doesn't matter, both are obtuse and guardians of their sister's virtue, suddenly one of them looms into sight from behind the rocks, like a jack-in-the-box, with outraged eyes and big clenched fists. I escape with a broken tooth, but I'm quite sure my opponent has a cracked rib, you can hear his moans in the sound of the waves, like a beached porpoise.

August 20

The night of the barn dance I hesitated a long time before joining in the fun. For a long time I gazed at the squat mass of the barn far off in the night, its small windows faintly lit by oil lamps. The square-dance music came out in loud bursts, stinging my arms and legs, ascending my spine. I finally decided to go in, a flask of home brew in my back pocket, my fine brown hat tilted over my ear, clad in arrogance from head to foot.

I slipped among the dancers like an eel. I took my place in the chain with the other men, bowed to my partner in the ladies' chain, and pretended not to recognize good old Maureen, her bulging eyes filled with compromising adoration. The stir caused by my arrival soon calmed down into whispering little waves and everyone was carried away by the dance, as by an equinoctial tide. Creaky fiddles and accordions were unleashed. A litter of puppies under the mother's belly wouldn't be more fraternal, closer, warmer, and huddled together than our little group of dancers in the sweltering heat of the barn, all except for my aunt Irene, who was sitting on her chair like a dead fish watching us whirl around like mayflies around a lamp. I touch Olivia's hand, I touch Nora's hand, I go from one to the other, I graze the fingers of my grandmother Felicity, or my aunt Yvonne, I move from hand to hand and as I go past I sense the sweet,

warm presence of fast-moving palms. Everyone without ex-
ception exudes the same hot, strong human smell, it steams
in our faces, mingles with laughter, blends with the perfume
of ripe hay behind the openwork partition. I swing Olivia,
my arm around her waist. She is as free and alone as she was
the other day amid the waves, the dance bears her and carries
her along in a perfect joy in which I have no part. I am struck
by an urge to reach Olivia, through ruse or violence, to exist
with her at the very heart of the magic circle of the dance,
where her little dancer's life is free and defenceless.

Nora won't have anything to do with me. Now she is listening very closely to the velvet voice of uncle Nicholas, most
likely telling her about the salvation of her soul. His clergyman's collar, his clergyman's black suit, his clergyman's
authority. The reverend gentleman is all red, and he wipes
his forehead with his handkerchief. The end of the evening
when the sandwiches and cakes are brought out is ruined by
Percival's howling that nothing can appease. What the idiot
has seen, only tears can express.

August 31, 1936

At the rate that things, and people, animals, the landscape,
are going, it seems right that the last day of summer is near.
Tomorrow I'll be far away, completely removed from this
place, from the people, the animals and the things of this
place, a free man again, on the road, using various means of
transportation that won't cost me a penny (all those big red
pennies earned in the service of the Widow Maureen Macdonald, née Brown), a sort of vagabond heading for Florida
with a precise magnetic compass in my head, pointed toward
the beaches and swamps of your native peninsula, old Mick.

My cousin Maureen doesn't suspect a thing. She's by my
side, knitting, while I write at the oilcloth-covered kitchen
table. She's turned the heel. Now she's decreasing for the
toe. She'll surely finish her second sock this evening, the first
being already done, soft and smooth. As soon as I have the
pair in hand it will be a pleasure to slip them on, before I

put on my traveling boots. As long as good old Maureen finishes them in time. I dream of those socks more than anything else in the world. She mustn't let go of her four clicking needles during Nora and Olivia's visit. The Atkins girls are paying visits now. They'll be here soon. Percival told us this morning. Already, since yesterday, Olivia's three men, probably wanting to put Olivia's good behavior to the test, have taken advantage of it to leave the family house. Patrick, his sailor's cap pulled well down over his dirty gray eyes, is jauntily sailing along the coasts, in search of smugglers. As for Olivia's father and her younger brother, Sidney, after spending the summer contemplating all sorts of men's affairs—buying a mower and fishing tackle, they specify—they've finally decided to go to Quebec. So that now the precious Olivia Atkins has, with a good deal of sound advice, been entrusted to Nora's parents for a few days.

I like knowing that Olivia and Nora are together in the same house, sharing the same occupations, sitting at the same table, like sisters, sleeping in the same bed like two nasturtiums in a container of cool earth. I like being able to sniff them in my dreams, both of them, under the sheets, their smell of girls, of sisters. Which of the two has the prettier breasts? If their slight souls were transparent, you could see me basking there, a passing stranger, wanting to cling to them, to destroy them most likely.

Though the season is ending, it didn't happen all at once. Throughout the month of August, between sunrise and sunset, there were some warnings that autumn was making its way, behind the horizon. Long before the storm, we were given a few little signs. First, an almost imperceptible change in the light, then long days of cold white tow. Fog you could cut with a knife. My aunt Irene took advantage of it to hang herself in the barn behind the rectory. That woman never seemed alive, her true nature was to be colorless, odorless, tasteless, already dead at birth. The hanging hasn't changed much, except that my uncle the minister can't keep her with him in the house now, he was quick to bury her in the earth with a great show of dignity, it appears, and some necessary prayers.

But I must tell you about the storm. A fine strong three-day storm, the kind I like. Rivers and streams overflowing, bridges and houses swept away, broken trees, devastated beaches, wharves ripped away. The papers talk about nothing else. I have a muddled recollection of a sort of drunkenness gradually taking hold of me as I gazed at the raging sea, reducing me to the role of a wisp of straw being carried away by fever, while a sort of song was forming in my veins to accompany the elemental fury. I spent most of my time on the beach. I was wild and free as the wind and through my mouth, my nose, I exhaled a great indestructible breath, very like the wind. The drunkenness I'm talking about had nothing to do with the demon rum, at least not in the beginning.

Torrential rain. For three days. The water no longer enters the earth. The village began to float like an island cast adrift with its mountain, its fields, its houses, its outbuildings, with no anchor or anything to hold them back. I took it into my head to live out the storm to the very end, as fully as possible, at the heart of its epicenter like the madman that I am, finding sensual pleasure in the fury of the sea, hurling myself at it, utterly weightless, like a cork. Chilled to the bone on my rock, in my wet clothes, I shout myself hoarse in the infernal roar. No one can hear me and the raucous cry that bursts from my throat does me good, frees me from an excitement that was hard to bear. The unleashed sea breaks on the shore, clashing into the rocks, throwing up a thick cloud of pebbles and bits of wood, of debris of all sorts. I return to Maureen's to dry off, to eat and sleep. Each time I appear I take a fresh pair of pants, a fresh shirt from the wardrobe of good old Maureen's late husband, then I go back to my post on my rock. Maureen yells that I'm crazy, that I'll catch my death. Nothing to be done, I must weep and howl in the storm, I must be stabbed to the bones by the rain and the spindrift. In them I find the expression of my innermost violence, my most secret life.

Exactly when did it occur to me to go and get the Atkins girls and take them out with me into the storm? I couldn't say. Already I'd started drinking to get warm and also for fear the great exaltation that held me so strongly would drop away. Not only was the effect of extreme excitement not blunted, but as I drank I acquired a sort of tender feeling for myself, as if I were holding in my hands my own uprooted heart, its warm throbbing now exposed, while the storm seethed all around me, without broaching my life's warm mystery, still intact.

Nora's parents' house in the night, the orange glow from the lighted windows, under gusts of rain. Earth and water can barely be distinguished one from the other. A single expanse of water as far as the eye can see. Nora's parents' house is moored in the middle of the sea. I walk on the water and reel in the wind. I arrive at the kitchen door and knock as hard as I can. From this moment I have only a fragmentary image of people and things. The fragments of people and things, on the other hand, take on an excessive importance, an extraordinary intensity, lit by several-hundred-watt bulbs. First of all my muddy shoes standing on the kitchen linoleum, the dirty water that streams off my shoes, the reprobation of the entire family concerning my shoes on the kitchen linoleum. I can't see their faces, but I can sense the reprobation of each and every one of them falling on me like a sledge-hammer. I don't even know if Nora and Olivia are among those assembled in the kitchen to judge and rebuke me. My aunt Alice's high-pitched voice telling me to sit down. The wooden chair comes up to meet my backside, slides under my buttocks, the weight of my body collapses onto the chair. Tonight I seem to weigh two hundred pounds. The table is there, close by, and I'd like to let my arms drop onto it, so as to shed them, no longer feel their weight hanging from my shoulders. As for my head, it seems to me that it's slowly ripening, that it hasn't yet attained its full size or its true weight. I just have to wait and then, when the time comes, I'll lay my head on the table, between my arms. I'll rest my dirty face on the tablecloth with its cross-stitch embroidery. Though I'm a man I can distinguish very clearly the little red and green crosses that decorate the tablecloth, as if I were looking through a magnifying glass. It's hard to say what I have to say and my tongue gets confused in my mouth. I talk of the sea and the storm, of the wild beauty of the sea and the storm, and I plead with Nora and Olivia to come out with me onto the shore, into the black night, to lose themselves with me in the midst of the great wild celebration of the storm. I pronounce both their names more or less distinctly, but I speak to them as if they were a single creature with two heads, four arms, four legs, and two hidden little sexes.

"Nora, Olivia, it's so beautiful outside, come and see, Nora, Olivia, come, I'll take you, the greatest show on earth, come on . . ."

Did I really see Olivia's face, her astonishment, or rather, her sorrow, stiffening above me as I slumped head first onto the table? The time it takes to sink into sleep and Nora's voice floats in the air, swoops onto my head, saying I'm a bastard and drunk as a skunk. But I seek in vain her little pointed face and her slight body, carried away as I am by the gloom.

After this business of the storm, I must come back to today, which is fine and clear. People all over the province are repairing the damage caused by the storm. The Griffin Creek mountain is hard, far away, compact and blue like stone, and you wouldn't suspect that it consists of a mass of green trees. The horizon, clear and pure and unencumbered, is crisp in the first autumn light. We eat supper together, good old Maureen and I. When the last bite is swallowed I insist she go back to her knitting. It's important I have my socks tomorrow at dawn.

A bit of a stroll by the seaside after supper. Ran into Bob Allen on the road. He bicycled down from Cap Sauvagine and he's been hanging around here for a few days now. We walk together with no apparent goal, while each step we take brings us closer to the Atkins girls. Although we're side by side at the edge of the road, without exchanging a word or a glance, we seem to be walking one behind the other on the crest of a wall. It's a matter of advancing in a straight line, each man for himself, toward the slowly moving shadow that freezes for a moment, then starts up, zigzagging, split in two, then is put together again in a single piece, increasingly clear and precise. The girls' white berets form patches in the twilight. Soon, Nora's cascading laughter.

Nora laughs too loud. Avoids looking at me. Only has eyes for Bob Allen. Lifts her laughing face to him. All four standing in the middle of the road. At first, we're awkward together, though soon a thousand little happy things, inexplicable, invisible, dart out of us, drift in the air, then panic and crackle, mingling with the insects' hum on either side of the road. It's a matter of making the space ahead of us last as far as Maureen's house. Boys and girls walk with noisy little steps, fill the countryside freely with heat, with laughter, with broken sounds, with living breaths. Our youth, the summer drawing to an end, surprise us no more than the sea air we're breathing.

Arrival of the Atkins girls at Maureen's, with their Sunday-best manners that exasperate me. I'd rather stay outside and watch the rising moon. While Bob Allen moves on, heading back to Cap Sauvagine.

The beach is deserted, my old rowboat fastened to a tire seems to be gliding across the shiny sea. I start to bail out the boat. I bathe in the orange light of the moon that's rising in the sky, swollen like a ripe fruit filled with moonbeams. My hands, my arms, my back, my face are exposed, each in turn, to the moon's evil spell. I remember the saying that a child who sleeps in the light of the moon risks an evil spell. The twins, Percival, and I must have spent a fair amount of time in the moonlight when we were little. The spell cast on us has produced three innocents and a human devil whom I must live with.

The sea laps softly, gleams in long fiery trails. My brother Percival is there, walking and waving his arms. The moon excites him, that's for sure, I'm afraid he'll start to cry. As for my uncle Nicholas, his gait on the sand is like that of a crab that doesn't know where to go. Since his wife's death he often wanders on the shore, by day or by night.

As soon as I've bailed out the boat I'll take the path that goes up to the road, wait for Nora and Olivia to come out of Maureen's house and greet them in the moonlight, hat in hand, something I've never done for anyone. Tomorrow when good old Maureen wakes up, I'll already be far away, on the road to Florida. I won't see her crumpled face and her great sad cow's eyes. It's better this way. I must remain light, clear of all worries or bad conscience, if I'm to undertake such a long journey.

I finish this letter on my knees, by the light of the moon, sitting in my boat. So long, old Mick.

THE BOOK OF NORA ATKINS

Summer 1936

laughs in torrents unchecked
at full force   at top speed   with abandon
and as she intends.

Hélène Cixous

YESTERDAY, JULY 14, I turned fifteen. A daughter of summer, I shimmer brightly from head to toe. My face, my arms, my legs, my belly with its patch of rust colored fur, my russet underarms, my auburn hair, the heart of my bones, the voice of my silence, I dwell in the sun as in a second skin.

Cock cries filter through the cretonne curtains, shatter on my bed in musky fragments. Day is beginning. At six o'clock the tide will be high. My grandmother has promised to come for me, with my cousin Olivia. The water will be so cold I'll hardly be able to move. Simply the pleasure of feeling alive, in the innermost heart of my being, at the chilly center of those things that surge out of the night, then I'll stretch, yawn, shudder, and seek light and warmth on the horizon.

I curl up in my bed. All around the house birds are cheeping. The forest so near. The blue spruce against the window. The shiny little black eyes of blackbirds and thrush peep out behind the curtains. Day is beginning. I've been fifteen years old since yesterday. My mother kissed me, like on New Year's Day. My grandmother gave me a green dress with a white angel-skin collar. My older brother, who's a pilot with Cunard, will come ashore at Quebec tomorrow on the *Empress of Britain*. He'll be here Sunday at the latest. He promised to bring me flasks of scent and cakes of soap.

I'm like a cat, my eyes barely open but already filled with all the energy in the world. I spring onto the floor. My bare feet feel the soft little rug, the smooth floor. I count the big knots and the little ones on the wooden partition, I see the washstand with its blue basin and white towels, the pitchers of water lined up on the floor, I inhale the light breathing of my sleeping sisters, each in her little iron bed, I listen to the whole attic humming with childlike breathing, the three girls on the left, on the right the three boys, a thin plank partition between them. I kiss my sister, the youngest one, without waking her, her round cheek, her fresh peony smell.

Here are my grandmother and my cousin Olivia waiting at the side of the road. I take an apple from the kitchen table, munch it outside in the wind and spit the seeds in all directions. Orchards will spring up to mark my passage through the countryside.

Felicity, my grandmother, awakens earlier every morning. Arriving before dawn sometimes, she takes Olivia and me through the darkness, the better to see the daybreak. Before the least ray appears on the horizon, when the night is no longer totally night, as it is becoming pale and sticky, clinging to our clothes, its chilly muzzle on our shoulders, we sit on a rock, my grandmother, Olivia and I, huddled together. Waiting for the light. The pallid hour takes us by surprise like a cluster of slippery seaweed stuck to a rock, soaked to the bone with the very temper of the night.

The first pink glimmer on the gray sea and my grandmother declares we must splash about in it right away, that it's the new soul of the sun unfurling on the waves.

When the high tide comes later, covering the shores in full daylight, Felicity stubbornly refuses to swim, becomes unsociable and distant. One must love her at dawn when she's tender and soft, set free from a spell.

I like days that are white with heat, when the water and sky reflect one another, a fine warm mist covers everything, and on the soft, oyster-colored sandbar, footsteps are erased as they are formed. The horizon is beyond our grasp. The earth's first day has not yet occurred. The seas have not yet been divided from the land. I'm six years old and I've gone out with my uncle John, who has just lifted his nets at low tide. Olivia and Percival are in the cart with us. The old horse's hooves sink into the mud, he drags them out, the water seethes, every step awakens a sleeping spring. Somewhere in the distance the muffled rumble of the rising tide that follows us in hurried ranks. As usual, uncle John's face is morose and impenetrable. He seems to fear neither devil nor tides—unless he's decided to drown us all, along with the horse and cart. The two big barrels in the cart are full of fish, still wriggling, with big eels struggling, dying, right beside us. Uncle John does nothing to urge on his horse, which sets down its hooves, then slowly lifts them with a squelching sound. There's something reassuring and monotonous in the horse's tranquil tread, his smooth attempt to get us out of the mud, and about my uncle's grumpy profile too, his hunched silhouette set against the sky, stubborn in his bad mood and his certainty that he's right.

The tide attacks us, not head-on but insidiously, from beneath, subterranean at first, then rising to the surface, lapping at the cartwheels and the horse's hooves. You need only follow the horse's legs sinking deeper, step by step, to measure the advancing tide, hooves, fetlocks, pasterns, shanks slowly disappear. In the time it takes to notice the sandbar now covered with a thin film of shuddering water, at the juncture of the approaching waves, the horse is in water up to his belly. Uncle John is a wizard. He need only flourish his whip toward the ground and immediately the ground comes closer. All of Griffin Creek looms up at the tip of uncle John's whip, with its white houses set askew on the hillside. My parents' house is the most comforting of all, recognizable by its carved wood gallery. Around us, the water is reformed, it spreads out in length, in width, in depth. The tide will be high around seven o'clock tonight. In an old cart drawn by an old horse led by a sullen man, Olivia, Percival, and I emerge from the high sea like sea creatures, bearing fresh fruits of the sea.

We knead wet clay in our hands to make bread. Olivia, Percival, and I are bakers. My grandmother is a dolphin. My mother and Olivia's mother knit. Here they are on the shore, in the shadow of the big pine, needles clicking, wool unwinding endlessly. Their full skirts spill over on all sides, almost completely hiding their canvas folding stools. Their faces, under straw hats, draw closer, whisper stories of birth and death. If I could hear them, and the silences here and there, I'd know everything a woman should know. But I'm still too young and the shadow of love that looms in mothers' conversations is secret and fearsome.

We make gray bread from clay and sea water. It runs down our hands, arms, and legs, cold and gray. The small loaves lined up on a board in the sun turn white and crumble. Percival says they're horse manure and that he's going to throw it on the road to fool the sparrows. I protest. Olivia protests. A steady battle ensues. Clumps of mud are thrown on both sides, fall on us, spatter us, making a flaccid sound. The mothers are on their feet now, with their straw hats, their knitting needles, and their balls of wool. Arms waving, they shout like mad creatures. Clouds of white birds swirl above their upraised arms.

There's a good reason why I play by the seaside so often. I was born there. It's as if I were seeking myself in the water and sand. I was made of the dust of the earth like Adam, not taken from between Adam's dry ribs, I am first as Adam was first, I am I, Nora Atkins, still damp from my singular birth, avid for all knowledge of land and of sea. In another life I could have lain a long time in the sea with no need to breathe, my lungs not yet opened out, like someone who stops up his earthly breathing and gives in to the delights of underwater existence. In vain my cousin Patrick keeps telling me, "Exhale into the water, inhale outside the water," I'll never learn the crawl like my cousin Olivia. It's too complicated. Divine ease underwater, my body filled with memory— I feel it still, in my dreams.

My cousin Percival is growing taller and heavier under our very eyes. He's becoming a giant. His face is the face of a little child that's been blown up like a balloon to force it to grow. When we fight, he arranges things so I win, "for fear of crushing me like a fly," he says. His clumsy hands seek my skin under my dress. This morning when I came out of the water, shouting from the cold, he caught me by the ankles and threw me down on the sand. The weight of his body on mine, his rough tongue on my salty cheeks. I struggle like a fish out of water. Percival licks my nose, my neck, my bare shoulders. But here's my grandmother top to toe, even taller than Percival, stronger than Percival, the very force of this earth. She rises above us, commands and orders, thunders and roars.

Percival starts to cry. I wipe my cheek, my nose, my shoulders, as if a big dog had been trying to lick me. As I look at Percival's puffy face, the trace of tears on his cheeks, I notice that my cousin has the beginning of a mustache. I start running toward my parents' house. My grandmother told me to, in a voice that would brook no argument.

Uncle John shouldn't have been told. Uncle John is mean. My grandmother told him everything, and uncle John whipped Percival, the way you whip a horse. Poor Percival, what can I do to console him without being devoured by him—his tongue, his teeth—like a lamb in his paws?

I like summer Sundays when the church door is wide open onto the countryside. The song of birds, the murmur of insects blends with the hymns, with the sound of the harmonium. Great odorous gusts enter on all sides, like waves in a heavy sea. The black bulk of my uncle Nicholas is authoritarian and reassuring. He talks about God and about the men and women of Griffin Creek who owe obedience to God and to him, uncle Nicholas, God's representative at Griffin Creek.

He thinks "I am the Lord's anointed," but his man's head is rust-colored, like mine. His unctuous gestures are those of a man attempting to please both the people of Griffin Creek and himself. The beauty of his voice is more overwhelming than any prayer. The words of the Reverend Nicholas Jones are taken from the Bible, he seizes them, makes them shudder and sing in his mouth, the mouth of a man of flesh and blood.

And the Word was made flesh and dwelt among us.

And I, Nora Atkins, I too was made flesh and I dwell among them, among my brothers and cousins in Griffin Creek.

The word in me has not been uttered or written down: it is only a secret murmuring in my veins. Given over to the metamorphoses of my age, I have been tossed and kneaded by briny water, my breasts have just settled on my ribs like two doves, the promise of ten or twelve children with ultramarine eyes nests in two small pockets in the hollow of my belly. I am fifteen years old. I am still dazzled by the brilliance of my new birth. The new Eve. I know about boys. That sting in the middle of their bodies, while I, I am hollow and moist. Waiting. Without undressing, obstructed by clothing, not even holding hands, the boys and I communicate already, through shudders, through hidden fever, while with our uncovered faces and our bare hands we smile and take on color in the light. Like the American at the general store the other morning. First of all, silence. Only our eyes. Then all our senses alerted, the throbbing of blood perceptible at ten paces. The man isn't handsome or good, his red tie, his gold tooth, and yet I kindle him from his feet to his head, like a torch that will not be fine or good, but necessary in the blaze of summer. (Somewhere in the countryside the law of light, sealed inside a hollow tree.) No, no, I won't let the American touch me, with his big hands or his soft mouth or . . . Lord, no. No, no, I won't allow it. I call him "dirty old man," but I'm laughing too hard for him to take me seriously. Uncle Nicholas slaps me hard and delivers me from the American. Uncle Nicholas is a brute. Beneath his exquisite exterior, his clerical collar, his smooth manners, there hides a dull brute. Percival is a big slobbering, whimpering dog. Oh God, don't let the first one be Percival who's an idiot, or uncle Nicholas who possesses the knowledge of good and evil, like the tree that stands in an earthly paradise.

Bob Allen, who comes from Cap Sauvagine, kissed me the other night, at dusk, on the deserted road, as I was coming home from cousin Maureen's. He kissed me on the mouth, the way a man kisses a woman. It made my whole body feel funny and nice, like gooseflesh. God, don't let the first one be Bob Allen. My mother says he goes with whores and that's why he's got bad breath. My mother knows everything.

Some day the love of my life, handsome and strong as a king, will walk down the road to Griffin Creek; I'll know him at once by his dazzling skin, his flawless heart, visible through his bare chest . . . He'll take my hand and make me his queen before all the inhabitants of Griffin Creek, who will gather by the roadside to hail us. I can hear it: Long live the king! Long live the queen! I'm wearing a crown and I'm trembling from the tips of my toes to the roots of my hair. I'll be the Cotton Queen or the Orange Queen, because he'll come from a distant land, where the sun always shines, night and day. I'll open the hard cotton pods and be submerged in soft white down. I'll swallow whole kumquats, heart and skin, bitter-sweet. I'll sleep on bales of cotton like clouds. The king of cotton and oranges will sleep with me, his shining crown and skin. We'll be husband and wife, king and queen, for all eternity. No, no, it's not Stevens.

When you look down from here it seems quite still, the surface scarcely wrinkled, though you know very well, from having looked at it so often from up close, what hollow depths, what snowy peaks are born and die at every moment on its vast back, in the wake of the wind and the motion that wells up from the abyss.

The Lord is my shepherd.

Better than a whiff of incense, the sea spray bathes the church, permeates the fir-wood stalls, and even our joined hands, with salt.

The sea from the distance, faintly curled on the surface, seemingly compact and calm beneath, yet from having known it since childhood all of us are aware of the deep rumbling at its heart, perceptible too at our wrists, steadfastly throbbing.

All the people assembled in the little church with their hands joined, their mouths open, sing and chant, feigning ignorance of the ebb and flow of their baptised souls.

Standing drenched in light, the black shadow of his hat over his eyes, Stevens has just appeared in the doorway. Starting now, things will happen very fast in Griffin Creek. Uncle

Nicholas, aunt Irene, Stevens, Percival, Olivia, and I, all will be swept along in the rush of our own blood, left behind in the countryside by the hot haste of life and of death.

Side by side on the same pew, her shoulder against mine, Olivia and I, both like children and lacking true speech, cling with all our might to the word of Scripture. Siamese twins since birth, never apart, filled with secrets unexpressed and sharing the wonder of life. It took just one glance, from the back of the church, at the two of us together, one person only, by an insolent lad, and then nothing between us was ever the same. I don't want Olivia with me now, following me like a shadow. I exist without her and she exists without me, and she has to learn that, my childhood sister who has been unhappy and too solemn, ever since she vowed obedience to her dying mother. "He's looking at me!" "No, at me!" More than any other words, these banal observations set us at odds and separate us forever. I'd stake my life on it, he was looking at me with his hooligan's eyes that emit rays from a distance, rays that pierce me through and through.

The hay is ripe. I've just examined a blade from very close, with the eye of a connoisseur. The slender green stem, its small mauve and silver head bursting with bloom like a cattail. I gather yarrow, vetch, and goldenrod all along the road. I make a big bouquet, with blades of hay for greenery. My grandmother receives my bouquet and the news that the hay is ripe, ready to be mown, with no apparent fuss, only her green gaze seems to soar above all things, accepting and blessing all things, even beyond the horizon.

Women and children follow the mower with big wooden rakes to sweep up the hay as it falls. The newly cut grass pricks my bare feet. In the cart, Olivia treads the hay, her legs and back swaying broadly with every forkful that falls. My uncle John has chopped up a long green gartersnake with his mower. When all the hay is mowed, both uncle John's and my father's, there'll be a barn dance amid the fresh aroma of new hay. It will be at our place because we have the biggest barn in Griffin Creek. Let's pray that it won't rain before all the hay is in.

By the end of the summer I'll have kissed them all, one after the other. This morning it was cousin Patrick's turn. It's all the same, I don't like the way he chews at my mouth and then right afterwards asks me if he's as good as Bob Allen. When it's Stevens's turn, I'll put my arms around his neck.

No, no, I won't. Stevens insulted me.

We make a lot of noise stamping our feet. The noise is part of the festivities, marking the rhythm. The old folks are out of breath from whirling around, and the young have red cheeks. All except aunt Irene. Her washed-out dress. Her faded eyes. The musicians are thirsty. Tony Brown, who totters when he walks, decides to bring them something to drink. A long lock of brilliantined hair falls across his nose. He pours beer in his hat and makes his way through the dancers, trying to push them back, his hands busy holding the hat with the beer spilling onto his trousers and the floor. The dance forms again around Tony, pressing in on him. The spilled beer is sticky underfoot. The musicians are still thirsty.

Stevens is showing off. When I dance with him I pretend I don't know him, though there's only one name in my head, Stevens, Stevens, Stevens. You have greatly offended me. I wish I could turn to ice when I dance with you, so I could freeze you too, from head to toe, like a dead snowman, you, your evil heart, your dreadful secrets. Instead, I'm on fire and I move from hand to hand, following the dance, melting like a candle.

In autumn when the snow geese leave this corner of the world by the thousands for more clement skies, I hear their honking up above the house, high up in the gloom. The perfect shadow of their formations passes through the shingled roof as if it were transparent and alights on my quilt, fleeting black geometry. I could touch with my hand. Lying on my bed, my sisters asleep in the enclosed room, my ears alert, I sense a sort of muffled barking far away. If I get up, barefoot, and lift the cretonne curtain, crane my neck and raise my head, I see the sky covered with birds in full flight, like regiments deployed by night. The evenly shaped v moves at the speed of the wind.

Back in the warmth of my bed, the sheets pulled up to my chin, eyes shut, I wonder which of these wild birds, under cover of what dense darkness, will alight on my roof one evening, in the course of its journey. A swan. I'm sure it will be a swan. His plumage will open, I'll see his naked heart, beating only for me. Then all at once he'll shed his white feathers, and they'll rise in a snowy mound at his feet. His form, that of a man set free from a spell that was crushing him. His face the pure face of a crowned king. No other girl in the world will be loved, will love, more than I, Nora Atkins. I dream. I sleep. Love. Unless he were to come by sea, from one of those passing foreign ships, decked out in every color, their poignant foghorns under clumps of cotton wool. He lands. He sets foot on the shore, takes me in his arms, carries me away, and nails me to the front of his pirate's ship. A figurehead for eternity, my small breasts frosted with salt, the waves slapping my face, and I can't wipe them away. Most likely he'll come along the yellow sandy road, in a cloud of dust. All the nickel on his car glittering in the sun. A Chevrolet or a Buick. What's important is that it's new and glistening, with soft cushions and a whining horn. Americans sometimes come like that, in summer, looking at us like strange animals while the beauty of our landscape seals their lips and freezes their souls.

It was on foot, making his way through the sand, like a tramp with his dusty boots and the bundle over his shoulder, that one fine morning Stevens arrived in our midst.

In the fall I'm the one who usually takes supplies to the hunters if they don't venture too deep into the forest. With a canvas bag laden with provisions on my shoulder, I walk into the little woods behind my cousin Maureen's house. My breath is visible in the cold air. A whiff of smoke between my teeth that warms my nose as it passes. I keep looking at my feet, for fear of falling. The fissured path is full of humps and hollows, dead branches and creaking leaves. In places it's all swamp. Or better yet, streams I must ford. I wade through the mud. Though I keep saying, to urge myself on, that in a moment I'll sniff, up close, the hunters' warm smell, the musky reek of carnivores lying in wait, I can't help thinking about my mother's warning.

"Be careful they don't mistake you for a deer in the woods . . . Your fawn-colored hair . . . Watch out for hunters, little girl."

Welcomed and feted by them all, shimmering shadows of blue on their prickly cheeks, their white teeth, their black nails, I offer the thermos of scalding coffee and greasy meat pies. We form a circle around the wood fire, shoulder to shoulder, for warmth. My uncle Nicholas, in a red-and-black checked mackinaw, his rifle over his shoulder, laughs harder than the others. He calls me his "kitten." It's as if any notion of ceremony had left him once he took off his cassock. My cousin Sidney offers me a drink of something colorless as water, which burns like pepper. My father, who's been looking highly displeased for a while now, tells me to go back to the house, right away.

This time it's summer, and I'm the "huntress." I walk cautiously over the pine needles. A bee buzzes around my head. I chase it away with a gentle wave of my hand. Mustn't rush things. Mustn't do anything to attract attention. My cousin Stevens is walking fifteen paces ahead of me. I've promised myself I'll track him till he turns around. Do nothing, now, to hasten this pivoting of his entire person, with legs that go on forever, or to exhaust my patience and my precautions, before I see once more his thin face, his pale, piercing eyes in the light. A branch cracks under my heel, Stevens turns around, leans his back against a tree, calmly watches me coming. In just an instant our roles have changed. Now he's the hunter while I tremble and plead, though I'm furious to be trembling and pleading in silence before him when it would be so easy to agree, like equals, equal in their desire.

"Don't do anything you'll be sorry for."

His disdainful manner. His eyes, blank as a statue's. His great carcass leaning against a fir tree. I think his hands are in his pockets. A moment more and he'll start to whistle. No, no, I won't put up with that. Insulting me to my face. I'll never forgive him. He refused to kiss me the way a man kisses a woman, and I've been waiting for him since morning, shadowing him like a hunting dog following a trail. Stevens's hard and handsome face, his long legs, his boy's sex hidden in his boy's clothes, his disdain, my fury.

I run till I'm out of breath. I wrench my ankles on moorings. I'd like to be picked up on a stretcher, carried away, taken care of, I'd like people to say prayers around me. I'll go and get my grandmother, I . . . No, I won't tell her anything . . . I walk on the shore, at the water's edge, barefoot, my running shoes tied around my neck. Little waves gently lick at my toes. I catch my breath. I keep walking, more slowly now. My footsteps slapping on water and sand. I think I'm starting to expect the event that will be my revenge on Stevens. An old nursery song I heard from the papists at Cap Sauvagine keeps going through my head as I walk, aimlessly, beside the water.

Promenons-nous dans le bois pendant que le loup n'y est pas.

I adjust my footsteps to the rhythm of the song. I walk on the shore, near the boathouse. I am waiting for the event to occur.

Le loup y est-y?

The wolf has uncle Nicholas's face, his black suit and corpulence, his confused manner, that of a man dedicated to God who is tempted by the demon, like Jesus on the mountain. He's seen that I'm angry and not in my normal state. I'm sure that excites him. He makes me go inside the boathouse, to talk to me, or so he says. I sit on an inverted rowboat that's under repair. I'm still angry as I look at uncle Nicholas, my eyes leveled at him like pistols.

"I hate cousin Stevens! I hate him!"

My uncle the preacher tells me I mustn't hate anybody. He's all red and sweaty as he says it. For a moment I thought he was going to kneel down and beg me not to hate anyone, in Jesus' name. He repeats, "nobody, nobody," in a voice both hoarse and tender, as if he were naming, very softly, something infinitely deserving of pity and tenderness that was hidden in his own preacher's heart. As of now I'm no longer angry. I become sympathetic and calm, sitting on my upside-down rowboat, waiting for what's going to happen. The preacher comes very close to me. He gets on his knees in the dust, the sand, the blades of dry grass and bits of wood. I let him do what he wants, his damp hands searching in my bodice, my nipples becoming hard under his fingers. God, is it possible that the first time will be this big holy man who . . . He buries his head in my lap, his arms hugging my legs. He calls me "Nora dear," says he's miserable. At that moment Percival shows his face, flattened against the little windowpane.

Percival runs along the shore. He's going to find aunt Irene and tell her in his incoherent language what he saw in the boathouse. Aunt Irene has been sleeping like the dead for so long now, she'll brush Percival aside and tell him to hurry on home.

Uncle Nicholas leapt to his feet. His heavy body creaks at the joints. He says that I'm wicked. He clenches his fists. He seems to want to hit me. He says that through me, sin has entered Griffin Creek.

Aunt Irene committed her own sin, at dawn, in the barn. Aunt Irene's sin is the gravest one of all, the one for which there's no forgiveness, the same one committed by Judas, who hanged himself like aunt Irene.

I was there with all the people of Griffin Creek when uncle Nicholas took aunt Irene down and carried her in his arms back to the rectory, stiff, her neck broken, arms and legs dangling, her braid swaying in the air like a dead snake.

My cousin Maureen gave all the flowers in her garden— geraniums, phlox, bleeding hearts, petunias, tiger lilies. I gathered armfuls of wildflowers. All for the burial of Irene Jones, hanged wife of the Reverend Nicholas Jones. I cried more than the other women in the village. The church was full of sniffling and throat-clearing mingled with the funeral songs. Uncle Nicholas insisted on solemnizing the death of his wife himself, following the standard ritual. But his beautiful voice was different, all broken and rough.

I hate uncle Nicholas as I hate Stevens.

My cousin didn't even put in an appearance, either at the church or the graveyard. Religious and family ceremonies put the fear of the Lord into Stevens.

From time to time Stevens goes to town with Bob Allen and Patrick. For the same reasons as Bob Allen and Patrick. My mother told me. If you ask me, Stevens doesn't like women, just the dirty things you can do with women. I did something dirty too, with the preacher, in the boathouse. To get even with Stevens. I was seething with rage. But the preacher was ravaged by fever. His big face paler than usual, the strawberry marks fainter on his cheeks. My nipples hardening in his consecrated fingers. God, what a sin! Hurry, God, give me a boy my own age who isn't married or a preacher. So my whole body feels funny and nice, from head to toe as it was intended to, and for the love of my entire soul, born with the same intention, in savage innocence.

Aunt Irene was made for unhappiness and she's dead. Peace to her gray ashes.

I was made for life. I don't think I'll ever die.

The storm has gone on now three days and three nights. Torrents of water poured down onto Griffin Creek from the black sky and the violet sea. With all that water the wind is unleashed, hollowing out eddies of air and rain, hurling up giant waves to charge at the rocks, to uproot trees, threatening to carry away everything in a hundred-mile radius.

My father's house is deeply rooted in the earth, solid and strong it defies the storm. I live in Noah's ark. I have two sisters and three brothers. We have provisions enough for a week. My cousin Olivia is here with us, safe with us. My mother has curly hair and a pointed chin like mine. She knows everything that goes on in Griffin Creek. It's not that she goes running around looking for news, the news arrives of itself, drawn by my mother. Doors are never locked here. One of my earliest memories is of the screen door to the kitchen swinging on the passing people, dogs, cats, flowers, vegetables, fruit, and blackflies, in the summer heat.

For a long time my father called me his "treasure trove for

pious souls." Now that I'm grown up he doesn't dare. It's my little sister Linda's turn. She's five years old and she laughs like a loony, her little round face all crumpled with laughter.

Sometimes when I'm too wrapped up in what I'm looking at, bending over an insect or a leaf, concentrating so as to capture the passing moment, my mother smiles and calls me a "pretty cloud." When I'm thinking hard about boys I hide in the hayloft, deep in the hay, far from my mother's magic eye.

My nose against the window, protected by the glass, water pouring over my face without wetting me, at the very heart of the deluge but safe in my transparent bubble, I watch for the violet flash that, here and there, lights up the devastated landscape. My cousin Olivia is at the other window, next to the door.

Looming out of the lightning's flash, a long silhouette staggers and reels, dislocated, disappears in the dark, appears again in the fiery sky, slips on the waterlogged path, gets up, is confused again, then clear once more, it comes closer and closer, then collapses on the kitchen steps.

Was it I who shouted? Or Olivia? A name moves from my bosom to my throat, then is choked on my lips.

"Stevens! It's Stevens!"

A sort of great bird bristling with rain collapses into the closest chair. Actually my father slips the chair under Stevens. His haggard look. His hair dripping onto his face, clinging like seaweed, his eyes paler than ever, bloodshot and filled with water—tears or rain?

My father says Stevens is drunk as a lord. If you ask me, he's possessed by the fury of the storm that pounds on his skin, stretched tight as a drum.

He speaks, barely audible words, he calls, is it me, is it Olivia, he pleads, confused prayers. Something about going out with him into the storm, about living and dying with him in an abyss.

Neither Olivia nor I saw Stevens's thin nakedness wet with rain. My parents took him into the next room, undressed him and dried him, put him to sleep in the big bed . . . He won't stay there though. Abruptly sober, he declares he has things to do outside, that he doesn't want to miss any of the storm, that it's the chance of a lifetime, an event that won't occur again for a long time.

That night, Olivia refuses to share my bed in the girls' room. She'd rather sleep on the floor, on the little rug, rolled up in a red Hudson Bay blanket with black bands. I get on her nerves as she gets on mine. Her agitated dreams against my bed, while I give way to sleep. I'd have liked so much to know whose bosom is prettier, Olivia's or mine. Rain, wind, waves. I sleep surrounded by the storm in my parents' house, watertight as a well-caulked hull.

There's a picture of me sitting on a log by the seaside. I'm laughing, and my hair's standing up on on my head, because of the wind. My parents bending over the picture. I, awaiting their verdict. My father says I have a headstrong chin. My mother insists that he say what he really thinks.

"Say it, say that she's pretty."

My father frowns. He's afraid I'll become vain. Prefers silence. Leaves the room without looking at me.

My cousin Maureen has the nicest garden in town. The geraniums in the noonday sun. They scent the air beyond the fence, as far as the road. The odor spurts between my fingers when I break a moist green stem. I won't wash my hands all day, to preserve as long as possible the scent of the geraniums my cousin gave me.

Maureen has never been so lavish with the flowers from her garden. For some time now she's been wearing lipstick too, and paying attention to her hair.

Bunches of white hydrangeas, green-centered, waiting for the first frost which will color them brownish pink, the tall border of pink and white phlox tangled by the bees, two gnarled wild apple trees with tiny acid fruit. My father has a habit of saying that this is a crazy country, with summer too short and winter too long and all the gardens doomed to early death.

The end of summer already. I go visiting with my cousin

Olivia. I have a dark brown coat; Olivia's is black. Our white crocheted berets are very pretty. Stevens has been working for Maureen since early summer. My mother says he sleeps in the barn, as a model servant should.

The moon rises, orange, in the sky. When Olivia and I leave Maureen's, the moon will most likely be high, all white, metallic, broad shafts of it spread upon the sea like a nocturnal sun, milky and pale. Stevens will surely have had time to bail out his rowboat. We met him on the way to Maureen's. Very preoccupied with the matter of bailing out his boat, which is filled with water from the recent rain. Stevens said hardly a word to us. Percival merely made faces at us when we passed on the road. Bob Allen told us he had to go back to Cap Sauvagine.

Tomorrow's the first of September. Back to school. It's my last year. Olivia already runs a household. Three men depend on her for food and drink, for cleaning and washing.

Summer's over.

THE BOOK OF PERCIVAL BROWN
AND OF SEVERAL OTHERS

Summer 1936

It is a tale told by an idiot, full of sound and fury.

Shakespeare

LIFT THE CURTAIN. The moon is there. In the window. Me.
Locked up in the house every night. Have to go to bed at
eight. Creak goes the key. Locked up in my room for the
night. Don't want to sleep. Want to yell. Because I'm locked
up. If I yell, they'll beat me. I yell because of the moon. I
sleep for a while because I'm locked up. Might as well sleep
in my bed. A nap, then back to the window. Because of the
moon. The curtain. My cheek on the cool, nearly wet windowpane. I saw the white moon through the cold glass. Want
to go out. A knack for opening a window. Slowly. Silently.
Hand too big. Easy does it. Very careful now. Hand feels
heavy. Swollen. The knob cool in my hand. Turn it slowly.
Click. Hold my breath. Listen: Is anyone coming? Someone
in my family might have heard the knob turn. The silence
of the house. My parents. Even awake on their chairs in the
kitchen, their faces like wood. Silent as dead wood. No, they're
both asleep now. In their bed. Breathing heavily. Like logs.
Through the nose, the mouth. Fretch, fretch, fretch, gr, gr,
gr. Their snores sound alike. Mixed together. Father and
mother. Make funny-sounding music. My twin sisters, not a
sound. Their breathing a gentle sigh. You might think they
aren't even breathing. Their blonde braids, nearly white, don't
breathe either. They sleep at the rectory now. Both of them,
Pat and Pam. Their blonde braids, nearly white. Their little
girls' mild manners. My twin sisters, mild, nearly white. Sleep
at the rectory. Wake up at the rectory. Wash the dishes at
the rectory. Scrub the rectory floors with a brush. On their
knees. Mend the minister's clothes. Light the minister's fire.
Cook stews, peel potatoes, at the rectory, rectory, rectory.
Always at the rectory. Ever since aunt Irene died because she

hanged herself in the barn. Parents glad their young daughters have moved to such a fine house. The finest in Griffin Creek. A portico. White pillars. Parlor. Shiny furniture. Shelves piled with books. Padded sofa, glossy black. Like a black horse, glossy. Blue glints. Bulging padding. Full of horsehair. Sunken black buttons. Angels in the cupboards. The devil down cellar. The minister, master of the rectory. High chief of the church on the hill. Tells fabulous stories every Sunday. About the son of Naim's widow, the blind man of Jericho, the healing of a withered hand, Jesus walking on the water. My head is full of the fabulous stories the minister reels off. Every Sunday. Ears and head crammed with strange happenings. Sometimes it makes me want to yell. No words to say what the fabulous stories do inside my head. Don't have enough words for ordinary life even. I have to yell. From joy or sorrow. An uncontrollable sound. It starts in my belly. Rises into my chest. Chokes me. Squirts into my mouth. Bursts into the open air. I can't stop it. A sound that digs a black hole in my bones, then flies up in the sky. A tiny invisible plow clears the way. In my hardest heart. Deep down inside me. To let out the yell. Shattered into a thousand fragments. I, too, shattered into a thousand fragments. By the passage of my yell. Through misty memory. The trembling present. *That the bones which thou hast broken may rejoice.* My warm hand warms the top of the handle, painted white. The white is peeling. You can see the iron, like little black claw marks, on the window handle. A strange car drives along the road. The iron is cold in my hot hand. "Your numb hand," says my mother. There's more to do than turn the handle. You have to push the window. Both sides. The left and right sides of the window. Open the two-sided window. Without a sound. The moon comes right into my room. Pours onto the floor in white pools, but transparent, liquid, like egg white, only not sticky, just transparent and white. My view. The broadest view in Griffin Creek. The strange car still driving past. The wide-open window. The whole bay visible, framed in the windowpane. A big boat. And a little one. The wrinkled water sparkles like sequins. Bubbly like ginger ale. The moon isn't a fat round orange like people say. The moon is flat, thin, like white paper. A white paper circle. A paper plate, round, white, shiny. Bright, as if there was a thousand-watt lamp behind the white paper. The white road. The strange car disappears. The sound of a motor in the distance, fading. The big boat is heading for the open sea. I like to watch it disappear, slipping away, powerful and big, along the horizon. The little boat is still there in the glimmering of the moon. Further out to sea than a while ago. It seems to have stopped. One end stands up, the other points down. I straddle the window. Stay there on the sill. On the second floor of the house. Legs dangling in space. I bathe in the liquid light. The moon freezes me through my pyjamas. I'm going to take off all my clothes. Danger of falling. Take a moonbath. Feel the cold of the moon on my boy's belly. Get dressed again right away. Balancing on the window. With both hands, warm the soft tender bird in the middle of my belly. Make it strong and hard. Yoo hoo, here I am, dressed in my pyjamas. Looking once more at the distant sea. The little boat is back from its trip out to sea, green rather than black, fifteen to eighteen feet long. Clear and precise against the sea. Lit by moonlight. Shut the window as cautiously as I opened it. Back in the warmth of my bed. Sleep. I must sleep. It's time for sleep. My drawn curtains. The flowers faded on the curtains. Can't see through the faded flowers and leaves on the curtains. I turn to the wall. Sleep. Dream of my brother Stevens, who's good to me. Tell him in my dream that I love him.

The house asleep. My parents asleep. I asleep. Not yelling now. Nothing violent in my dreams. Utter sweetness. A blue-green world where I suck my thumb in peace. All exits barred. Cars and boats can't reach me here. My knees to my chin. Drowned in sleep. Sleeping water over my head. The infinite protection of the sleeping water. Several walls of water between moonlit Griffin Creek and me. My sleep shut tight as an egg, with me in the center. My room locked. The window shut. The cretonne curtain drawn across the glass. The wooden walls, the shingled roof of the closed house of my father, John Brown, husband of my mother Beatrice Brown. The night air in bright layers because of the moon, slips onto the roof. Nothing touches me now. I'm sheltered here. While the savage beauty of the nighttime landscape spreads out all around the house.

The inhabitants of Griffin Creek were alerted, one after another, in their first sleep. First of all Alice Atkins, her hair curly, her chin pointed like her daughter Nora's, awakens, concerned, says the girls haven't come in yet. Her husband, Ben Atkins, emerges with difficulty from sleep, slowly wrinkles his brow, his calm, sleeping face having trouble, it seems, assuming any expression at all. Looks at the alarm clock on the night table. Half-past eleven. The tick-tock fills the bedroom with a deafening noise. The girls left at half-past seven. To go to Maureen's.

Maureen's velvet gaze resting on the clock, apparently seeing nothing. The twelve strokes of midnight have just sounded somewhere in the empty house. Immeasurable fatigue in her back, arms, legs. Her head most of all. Standing in the middle of the kitchen, fully dressed, not having gone to bed, having waited so long for Stevens, she pulls down her sleeves as if she's just washed her hands, repeats to herself Stevens's last words, how long ago now, an eternity most likely. Maureen's entire body has had time to harden, turn to ice. Something intolerable has caused this hardening of her entire being, petrified. If she moves only her little finger now, she will shatter in a thousand pieces, like a bottle under boiling water. The words will remain intact, will never break, will resist the shattering of nerves, the bursting into tears, the passing of time. The words he hurled at her this evening from the threshold, through the screen door, not even taking the trouble to enter. So many stones to kill her in the dark. It can't be said that she saw his face, only his mouth curled over white teeth. His hoarse breathing in the night.

"I'm leaving now. Going back to Florida. Tomorrow I'll be far away. Poor Maureen. You're too old. Too old for me."

Stevens went to get his things from the barn. His long strides even faster than usual. His bare head.

Someone pounding. Harder and harder. Nearer and nearer. On my head, my chest, all over my body. To get me out of bed. My sleep broken by force. I was hiding in my sleep, now I'm pulled from my sleep by force, by the pounding. Somewhere else now, outside my body. Exasperated banging. Sleep clings to my skin. In sticky threads. Can't open my eyes. My ear, sharper and sharper, clearly makes out the pounding at the kitchen door. A volley. I sit up in my bed. Emerge from the mud. Downstairs, the sound of bare feet, rushing. My father's voice. A confusion of many voices responding to my father's voice. The slamming door. Once again, my father's bare feet. My mother's bare feet accompany my father's. From the kitchen to the parents' bedroom. Pause. They're talking softly. Parents' secret language in the dark of their big bed, as usual, most likely. Sometimes they argue, and their voices rise. Tonight they're whispering. Then comes a commotion as if it were morning. My father's feet in shoes, moving away toward the kitchen door. The door opens, then slams shut. He shouts through the screen door.

"I'll go have a look, then I'll come back and tell you."

I start to yell for my mother to open my door. Slowly she climbs the stairs, stopping at every step. As if every step that she takes on the stairs is oppressive.

Everyone's outside in the middle of the night, snatched from sleep, interrogated, questioned, pulled to their feet, clothed and shod, dropped into the landscape. Hands cupped around their mouths to call Nora and Olivia. Search for them everywhere along the main road, along ditches, in bushes, on the shore, in the boathouse, along paths and shortcuts. Our flashlights shine on this side and that. The few drivers who pass in their unfamiliar cars are shouted at, bombarded with questions. A few people from Cap Sec and Cap Sauvagine join in our search. Stevens has already found a way to inform Bob Allen at Cap Sauvagine. Bob Allen seems completely dazed. You can see his striped pyjamas under his open jacket. Patrick, scarcely disembarked from the *North Star*, has a mean look and a blue beard. He swears that never again will he leave Olivia unsupervised at her cousin Nora's.

At Maureen's house all the windows are lighted, from top to bottom, as if there were a fire. People crowd around her. No one sits down, and she asks no one to sit. She stands in the middle of the room, arms at her sides. All her strength concentrated, to keep from falling. Wavering even in her stillness. It would take nothing to make her collapse. Too deep a breath. The movement of a hair. A blink. She repeats that the girls arrived at her house around half-past seven and that they left at half-past nine. Bob Allen says that Stevens and he walked with Nora and Olivia to Maureen's, then parted on the road. Stevens refuses to enter Maureen's kitchen. However, he confirms Bob Allen's statement. Says he hasn't seen the cousins since.

No, no, it's not Stevens. I don't recognize him now. It's not Stevens. He isn't wearing his hat. His eyes, faded like a faded blue shirt, are constantly moving, as if he wanted to look everywhere at once, never settling on anything. Refuses to enter Maureen's house. Calls Nora and Olivia very loud, all over the countryside. Doesn't see me. Doesn't put his hand on my head as he usually does. Has certainly just washed his face and hands. Shaved too, perhaps. His cheeks smooth as if he's just come out of cold water, and somewhat pink. The hollows in his cheeks deeper than ever. His clean shirt. Stevens says "Bob and I." Repeats that they left Nora and Olivia at Maureen's. At the foot of Maureen's steps. Half-past seven, half-past seven, half-past seven, like a cuckoo craning his neck and repeating the time three times. Bob Allen also says half-past seven. Maureen too, without moving from her place. And she adds that half-past nine was when Nora and Olivia left her house. Maureen slumps into a chair. Says she has a terrible headache. I think I hear her beg them not to let Stevens come in. Stevens, standing outside on his long legs, leaning against Maureen's doorpost, moves off with abrupt little steps. Isn't wearing his brown hat now. His hair, slicked-down and combed, pasted to his skull.

I yell with impunity into the great open space of the night, facing the sea. Never have I had so much space and the whole night to inhabit with my cries. I shout with the others. Joined with the others. "Nora and Olivia." Shout with pleasure at first. My voice pushed to the outer limits of a living voice. Power set free in my throat and chest. The shout ricochets off rocks. My whole being emerges in my shouts. My shouts go beyond my body, through my body, reaching people, rocks, and sea. A little more and Nora and Olivia will no longer be uttered by me at all. Soon it will be a pure howl, without distinct words. Rending my chest. Howl for all those of Griffin Creek who are with me, who still utter clearly, "Nora Olivia," who call out too softly, who if they are to express terror require, more than any distinct syllable, the deep, inchoate scream of a calling beast. I think the moon is setting; it's going to disappear. After the moon and before the sun, the sky is sad as death. Between moon and sun slips that dark hour, pitch-black and gummy and more poignant than dusk. If Nora and Olivia are found there, hidden in the gray dawn, ten feet from us, we couldn't even see them. I think I'm crying now. My throat burns from screaming so much. I watch for the first ray of dawn on the sea. Perhaps my grandmother Felicity will appear in that first ray. Perhaps she will walk on the water in her red-and-brown bathrobe. She need only dip into the bathrobe's big pockets and take out her two granddaughters. Shrunk to the size of flies, they will grow as we watch, escaping any evil spell. They won't be lost then, but with us, alive. Their tangled hair, their summer dresses, their odor of ferns or of blood, depending on the day. Above all, their smiles. Their wet teeth. Ah! The first thing I saw when I came to the shore was Stevens's boat tied to its post in the sand. The water laps gently at the side of Stevens's boat. Oars crossed on the seats, as usual. Everything as usual, except that Nora and Olivia are lost. Ah!

The child shouts too loud. He should be brought home to his parents, put to sleep in his bed. With him, our anguish reaches a climax that's hard to bear. Those who've gone inland by car to Cap Sec or Rivière Bleue return one by one, with no news. Say it's better to wait until day before questioning people. But first, put that child to bed. Shut him up in his room. His father grabs him by the arm. Someone says it's better to let him eat before taking him away. Someone else observes that "that child" is fifteen years old and strong as an ox.

My grandmother Felicity is the same as always. No change in her behavior. She tries hard to stay the same so nothing else in Griffin Creek will change. In the hope that nothing else in Griffin Creek has changed already. She's just put more wood in the stove than usual, made a bigger fire, a bigger pile of toast, she's taken the big coffeepot from the cupboard, cooked a good two dozen eggs and several packages of bacon. I count three times ten people around the table. I eat from my lap, sitting on a packing case near the door. My twin sisters sit on the floor, backs to the wall, knees drawn up to their chins. You can see their white pants. My uncle Nicholas who's a minister says we'll have to write up the notice for the police. Someone says he saw a strange car drive down the road between nine and ten o'clock. No, no, I won't say anything, not about the strange car, or the big boat, or the little one. Too scared I'll be scolded because I wanted to go out at night, through the window. Locked up to sleep every night. I wanted to straddle the window. To jump into space. Gathered speed. Too high. Scared I'd break my legs. Scared I'd be scolded. A diffuse sulphur-colored light spreads over the countryside. Nora's mother trembles slightly, as if she had a fever.

It's in the papers. In big and little letters. English papers. French papers. Uncle Nicholas's notice is printed in the papers. My father reads aloud, following every line with his finger.

> *Disappearance of two cousins at Griffin Creek. Olivia Atkins, age 17, 112 pounds, tall, slim, elegant, blue skirt with narrow pleats, white sweater, black coat, white shoes, white crocheted*

beret, blonde hair, blue eyes. Nora Atkins, age 15, 102 pounds,
frail, elegant, pink dress, brown coat, white running shoes,
white crocheted beret, auburn hair, blue eyes.

Blue eyes everywhere in Griffin Creek. In every garden. Every
tree. They grow like blue fruit. Just hold out your hand.
Nora's eyes, Olivia's eyes hidden among blue fruits. Unless . . . On the shore mixed in with the agates in the sand.
Drops of water solid now, water-stones. I'll go to the seaside
and gather the blue eyes of my cousins who are lost, with
their coats, their girls' skirts, their smell of ferns and blood.
Locked up in my room once again I have no voice. To yell.
I moan very softly. An idiot's song. Very softly. A sad murmur
in rhythm with my heavy heart. Tick tick tick tick. My heart
huge in my chest pounds against the bars. My heavy heart
could break everything inside me. If I'm not careful. Want
to get out of here. My parents turn a deaf ear. Too many
people downstairs. Endlessly entering and leaving. The door
slams. Tangled conversations. Strange voices blending with
familiar ones. Stevens's voice muffled as if he were talking
with his hands over his face. Men's clothes, nailed boots, soft
hats, reek of tobacco, a whole mob of strange men. In my
parents' kitchen. I sniff them under my bedroom door, through
the keyhole. Wish I could drive away the strange smells. So
they'd disappear, with their strange suits, their strange hats
and shoes. It stinks in the kitchen. And my parents put up
with it, though they're so clean and tidy. Usually.

We, the people of Griffin Creek, having been left behind by events, are unable to follow any longer, we are overwhelmed by the disappearance of Nora and Olivia and have no time for the necessary cross-checking among ourselves, we've been made to confront the police and charged with replying, without having time to consult among ourselves and think things over. Stress the route taken by the strange car, to gain time. Try to understand. Delve more deeply. Put together all the pieces of the story. As a family. With no witnesses. Stevens has returned to his father and mother. It was best, in the circumstances. Going back to Florida was out of the question. Present a picture of united families. Stevens with his parents, whom he should never have left. Maureen in her widow's house, busy mending her widow's clothes and baking cakes if she so fancies. It's she who brings in the wood now and kills her own rabbits. It's not appropriate for Stevens to stay with her. Maureen was the last person to see the girls on the night of August 31. Gave them hot fudge and probably some of the sour apples from her gnarled trees.

His faded eyes wide open, like pools, his head bare, which is new, never seen before, its blond nudity surprising. My brother Stevens has no hat now. He sits on a straight-backed chair, his elbows on the table. Opposite him, a stinking stranger with a dirty bow tie. Too fat, face and hands too soft, glistening with oil. With my jackknife I could scrape away all the lard, down to the bone. We'll see. Too much skin now, flaccid and glistening. Can't put a human face and human hands back together. Rind. To be thrown to the dog. Now he's looking at me, severely, as if he suspects what I've just done to his fat, soft body with my jackknife. I'll say nothing. About the jackknife. Or the big boat and the little one. Or the strange car. Or Stevens's lost hat. The man keeps looking at me as if he was looking inside my head for the jackknife, the car, the big boat and the little one, Stevens's hat, everything that's hidden inside my head and keeps me from sleeping. Stevens leans across the table, swallows, says he's tired. Repeats for the tenth time, very softly, swallowing his words.

"Bob Allen and I walked the girls down the road to Maureen's. Bob Allen went back to Cap Sauvagine. Bailed out my boat. Met the minister on the shore. Had a smoke with him. Talked about salmon fishing, which has been prohibited since the end of June. Went back to my parents'. Didn't see the girls again."

The stranger's pointed little eyes seem to want to pop out of his head. His thin mouth reveals tiny green teeth. His words come out slimy and stained with green.

"What time was it when you went back to your parents' house?"

My father, more stooped than ever, arms too long, his hair

standing on end. My mother chillier than usual. Hard white snow on her hands and face. My parents, not looking at one another, say that Stevens came in around nine o'clock.

This is unbearable. I think I'm going to scream.

Our houses are no safer now than if they had no doors or windows, we are constantly being visited, invaded, questioned, and forced. The police are staying at White's Hotel not far from the village. At every hour of the day or night they come bursting into our houses, trying to catch us out, we the people of Griffin Creek who are already under a curse. The two plainclothes policemen with their trench coats and soft hats should pay a little more attention to what's happening elsewhere than here, on the main roads traveled by strange cars, they should set traps at the American and Canadian borders, interrogate everyone at the gas stations. Someone else is seeing to all that—cars, border, gas stations—they maintain, as they enter our houses without knocking or wiping their feet, clicking their heels. There are three policemen. Plus Chief Leroux who comes from Quebec City from time to time.

Police reports arrive from all sides. Our old trucks set out along the sandy roads, the steep hills, the late summer sun, the fog ever denser and whiter. Stevens, his father, Patrick, and Sidney, rush onto the road at any hour of the day or night to check the news as it develops. They've been seen at Rivière Bleue, radiant, in a green Studebaker, between two Americans. The smaller one had her head on the shoulder of one of the Americans. They were smoking Players or Turrets. All four went into the hotel at Rivière Bleue, amid much laughter. As soon as someone actually saw them, it was obvious it wasn't the girls. Bigger, older, more impudent. Makeup and dyed hair. No possible mistake. Furious at being disturbed in the hotel with their boyfriends, the green Studebaker parked opposite the hotel with its New Jersey plates, the two women treated us to insults.

The Atkins girls are no more to be found anywhere in the province than in the palms of our hands.

Rumors reach our houses, whispered as late at night as possible, when we're among adults, the children in bed and the police back in their hotel. Going over for our own purposes how each and every one of us accounted for his time on the night of August 31.

The policeman, the fat one, the one I cut the fat off with my jackknife, is doing all right now. Is resuming his old shape in the brisk autumn air. Fat and glistening in his dirty trench-coat. He smells like a toilet. I plug my nose when he comes in the house. Tell my brother Stevens so he'll be careful too. He laughs. Laughing is good for him. Afterwards, his jaw's not clenched so tight. His cheeks not so hollow. Ran his hand over my head as he used to. And I rubbed my head against his hand as I did before August 31. August 31. Last day of summer. Last day of the world perhaps. What if all of us from Griffin Creek have been living since then stunned, like old horses, not knowing we're dead? The two policemen, the fat one and the skinny one, gave orders to let me run around anywhere, as if I were a dog that could follow trails.

I run barefoot on the shore, to the edge of the waves. The cold little tongues of the waves lick my ankles. Nora runs ahead of me. I'm sure it's Nora. Her fire-colored hair tangled in the wind. With long strides she disappears ahead of me. For a moment a bright flame drifts above the waves. Then nothing. Nora extinguished like a light. Blown out like a candle. I closed my hands around a dead light. A bird flown away. Absence. The past, lost. I cry all along the road back to the house. The fat policeman waiting for me on the steps. Offers me mints. Asks me to tell him everything. My grief and my sorrow. Then, abruptly, he sticks his fat shiny face close to mine, talks to me with his pointed tongue showing over his green teeth, asks me if it's true that Stevens slept at home the night of August 31. I cry even louder. Repeat very softly that Nora was russet as an Irish setter, that she leapt about like an Irish setter and now she's lost.

My parents swear they locked me in my room at precisely eight o'clock on the night of August 31. As usual.

Climbed up on the cord of wood. Looked in the little parlor window. Saw the fat policeman questioning my uncle Nicholas, the minister. Saw uncle Nicholas standing in the parlor. His large size compressed, his big head even closer to his shoulders than usual. Still impressive though. Sacred. In his presence everyone stands, respectful. That stinking policeman is sitting in the minister's presence. Dares to sit down when the minister stands. The tub of lard I've already obliterated is looking at the minister insolently. Planted comfortably in his straw-bottomed chair. In the little parlor. I rap at the window so they'll open it. It wasn't shut properly and opens by itself. I must be invisible. Disturb nothing and no one. The scene continues, as if nothing had happened between my uncle Nicholas and the detective. My uncle's beautiful voice, made for casting a spell over people, seems to have no effect on the tub of lard.

"Met Stevens on the shore. Chatted with him for a bit. Came home. Went to bed very early. Read in bed."

The policeman squirms on his chair. As if the straw is pricking his backside.

"What time did you come home?"

"Around nine."

The policeman leaps from his chair as if the straw were on fire under his rear end.

"Amazing! Every person in this village who was outside on the night of August 31 came home on the stroke of nine, like a single man."

The idea of a single man makes me laugh as if I were seeing, end to end, uncle Nicholas, Stevens, Bob Allen, and the others braided together like garlic, pearly white.

My laughing upsets the policeman. He raises his head to the window.

"Scram, you little jerk."

Instead, I bend down and pretend to disappear. Then I show myself again, just my eyes, and see my twin sisters coming to testify, with their blue aprons and blonde braids.

They talk one after the other in voices so similar it's hard to know which is which. They say the same things too, in a steady, stubborn voice.

"The minister came home at nine o'clock."

One of the twins, however, suddenly draws away from her sister, advances a few steps, weighed down by a secret she can't contain. Fascinated by the absolute authority of the detective facing her. My uncle's authority suddenly no longer holds any weight.

"I'd gone to bed. Tossing and turning. Couldn't sleep. Had too much pork at supper. Too much moonlight through the curtains. Heard shouting outside. Chilling cries. Thought they were cats that . . . No, no, not cats."

The detective's voice becomes soft, almost tender.

"What time was it?"

"Don't know. I don't know. It was too dark to see the alarm clock."

"Had the minister come in when you heard this crying?"

Frightened by something in the very air she is breathing, Pam recoils. Stands with her twin. Carefully aligns herself with her on the little rug. Answers very quickly, out of breath.

"Yes, yes, yes."

Busy reading Malachi, his favorite of the twelve minor prophets, uncle Nicholas has heard nothing. Nor did my other twin sister, who was asleep at the time.

I run on the shore. My shoes full of sand. Sit down to empty them. Level with the waves. See the foam rise. Burst. White sprays. Shattered. White mist in the sky. Birds come out of the sea white with foam. Take flight in the gray sky. September. Feathers white with foam. Gray feathers. Yellow strands of gannets. Birds of the white foam. Born on the foam-white sea. Their piercing cries born of the waves. Their tough beaks bore into the waves, then emerge from the water. Mad birds shatter their watery shell. To be born anew. Filling the sky with heart-rending shrieks. Whirl about my head. Burst my ears. My shoes empty now. Still I sit on the wet sand. Thinking hard about my cousins Nora and Olivia, who are lost. And what if my grandmother, one fine morning. While everyone slept in the houses. Had taken them both out to sea? To lose them. Drown them like kittens? The high sea on the horizon. Its deep belly of water and sand. Its well-kept secrets. Live fish, dead beasts, drifting, skeletons of boats, black water-weeds, yellow, purple and green ones, its marine landscapes, green water pathways and roads, its beds of pebbles and sand, its tables of stone. Ah! I have no more breath. A long drawn-out sound. Rest my head on my knees. Weep into the wind. Deafened by the cry of the birds. They'll go away in squawking flocks. Soon. To Florida. My brother Stevens with them. My brother Stevens only passing through here, with us, the people of Griffin Creek. Just for the summer. Like the squawking birds. His dark brown hat lost at the bottom of our sea. He'll return along the roads, the way he came. His little bundle over his shoulder. His bare blond head exposed to sun and rain and autumn cold. With no more shelter in him than a bare hand in the fire.

Bob Allen is interrogated and questioned at Cap Sauvagine, in his parents' house just outside the village. Cold-leafed lilacs on either side of the front door. In the kitchen, the finest woodstove on the coast, huge, signed Eatonia. Polished steel, ceramic tiles, nickel, and mirror. Bob Allen's mother is with her son. Her large smooth bosom under a flowered bodice, her good big backside under a flowery skirt. Her pink face. Her hair straight as broom straw. As the policeman watches, attentive, she has just put a spice cake in the oven.

The policeman, the skinny one who's not so bad, sniffs the cake, rocks on his chair at the risk of scuffing the freshly waxed linoleum. Bob Allen stands rigid before the detective, like a little boy being scolded. He repeats that he walked to Maureen's with Nora and Olivia and that Stevens was with them. Then he got back on his bicycle and returned to Cap Sauvagine.

"Spent part of the evening with Jeremy Lord, the store-keeper, brought back the barrel of nails on my rack that my father'd asked for."

As for the time of his return, Bob Allen doesn't remember very clearly. He drops his head. His cheeks and ears are hot and red.

Bob Allen's mother has just taken the cake from the oven. The fragrance is so strong it softens the policeman. He still persists though, his voice less certain.

"What time did you come home?"

Silence from Bob Allen, who can only breathe in the cake's aroma that spreads through the kitchen. The policeman's voice sounds distant and utterly unimportant.

Mrs. Allen turns out her cake onto a chipped white plate.

No one is speaking now. The silence is filled with the aroma of batter and spices. The policeman's smooth voice repeats,

"What time did you come home?"

Bob Allen does not reply but looks inquiringly at his mother. Mrs. Allen offers the policeman a piece of cake, declares that her son came home around ten. He brought the nails his father had asked for. Went to bed right away, in the little bedroom off the kitchen.

The policeman swallows greedily.

Eyes half-shut, mouth full, Bob Allen gazes gratefully at his mother. Her oddly straight short hair, the aroma of warm cake on her skin. Huge, edible, nourishing, his mother protects him and keeps him. Bob Allen recounts in a thin voice that he took leave of Nora and Olivia at Maureen Brown's door and didn't see them again.

"What time was that?"

"Around seven-thirty."

"And then?"

"Stevens told me he was going to bail out his flatboat on the shore. I rode my bike back to Cap Sauvagine. Spent some time with Jeremy Lord."

The detective with his argyle socks and heavy shoes and gnarled hands asks for another piece of cake. He eats slowly now, apparently without tasting, mulling over the report he'll make to his colleague tonight at White's Hotel.

It's turning cold. Tonight the frost touched Maureen's hydrangeas. The heavy bunches near the ground along the gallery have turned pink and brown.

This constant coming and going of men, women, children and the dogs that accompany them. The people of Griffin Creek are going from door to door all through the countryside.

"Have you seen Nora and Olivia Atkins, our cousins, our sisters, our daughters, who disappeared on August 31?"

In French, in English, the same question, relentless, obsessive. While the leaves begin to fall, while the ground becomes harder under our feet. Then the terror advances.

But who shall abide the day of his coming? And who shall stand when he appeareth?

The little church in Griffin Creek is filled with the sound of our prayers. The minister's voice grows hoarse, like an old drunkard's. The words of the prophets pass through the minister's ruined voice. In the holy books they talk about Griffin Creek.

I laid his mountains and his heritage waste for the dragons of the wilderness. And now, I pray you, beseech God that he will be gracious unto us.

Who will be gracious unto us, Percival wonders, hands joined, eyes seeming frozen in his round face, and who can soften the terrible face of God?

Darkness arrives earlier and earlier. Faster and faster. Eager to devour the day. A sort of black mantle drawn over us. A cage of green and blue birds abruptly covered by a black cloth. After supper. The last bit of food swallowed. Slam, it's night. No more turning key. No more closed door. I go to sleep when I want. I go up and down the stairs, in and out of the house as I wish. My parents notice nothing. They're busy doing nothing, sitting in their chairs. Not a word between them. Not a gesture. And they're both full to bursting with thoughts that are hard to bear. They inhale quickly. As if short of breath. If the two policemen interrogate them (the one who smells like a toilet and the other who smells of Listerine), you'd think my parents had lost their memory. Little yes's, little no's, don't knows, deep silences. As for my brother Stevens, from repeating the same thing he seems to no longer believe what he says.

Break out of the house all alone in the dark. No one notices. Feel the darkness open as I pass. Like the sea under the stem of a boat. Taste the night on my face. My hands. Feel the night dissolve in black droplets on my clothes. The air filled with echoes like a cave. Call to Nora and Olivia. My calls swallowed by the deep night before they touch the ground. Snatched up by the silence as soon as they're born. A huge sphinx hidden in the black night, eater of language and cries. Simply meeting the fat greasy detective on the road makes me vomit. I spew him up there, in the stream, the stinking man with his bow tie. The sight of the rotten devil makes me puke. Yet he keeps walking through the dark as if nothing had happened. His short legs, his short arms jut out of his body. Now he has disappeared on the road. A taste of gall lingers in my mouth. I wipe my mouth with dead leaves. The stagnant taste of dead leaves in my mouth. More tolerable than the fat detective's stench. Though I vomited him into the stream at the roadside, Jack McKenna's still alive. Preparing to get into his green car and drive to Cap Sauvagine.

Olivia's house lit up in the night. Olivia's men are awake. Not waiting motionless on kitchen chairs. But entering and leaving the house. Going out to find out what's happening. Then returning. And setting out once more. Calling to one another. Criticizing one another for not supervising Olivia more closely. Their bearded faces are captured as they pass by the harsh light of the bulb over the door, then straightaway are swallowed by the gloom . . .

There shall be weeping and gnashing of teeth, declares uncle Nicholas.

I, Percival, in the dark regions of night, I hear the shadows creaking all around me. My cousin Patrick's truck creaks too, in the night; it stamps and moans although it's stopped at the bottom of the steps. The harsh glare of the lightbulb sways on the truck's shiny hood. My cousin Patrick flashes the lights of his old yellow truck. Two long streaks of white light are given off by the truck, fill with insects that sputter and rise up in clouds. Like snow. My cousin Patrick talks loud, his head half out of the truck, his hair full of white light and whirling insects. My cousin Sidney, in the light of the bulb over the door, shouts something about Nora and Olivia. But the night immediately swallows Sidney and Patrick's words. I don't understand. If Olivia's father is really standing now under the bare bulb, vociferating and shouting himself hoarse, I'm dreaming that I hear his big gruff voice declare that if his daughter's not returned to him, he won't answer any more questions.

Olivia's men are furious cats. They spit and their eyes glow in the night. One of my twin sisters heard cats crying on the night of August 31. God, what if it was . . . Crying is useless.

My tears would vanish straightaway into the wet black sandy substance that pours from the night. Better to walk around Olivia's house without a sound. Stick my face against the lighted windows. Sniff the new cement under the summer kitchen. Perhaps Olivia is being held prisoner. Tied up with rope. Too many men for just one girl isn't normal. They made her take a vow. Made her silent as a statue, her hair foaming on either side of her silent face. I've been rapping on the basement window for a long time now. Somewhere in the night I hear my voice yelling. Outside my body. Very far from me. Separate from me. Like the living head of a fish that's been cut away from its body. With a single stroke of the knife. On the close-cut grass, the sparkle of splinters of glass. My fingers. Cut. I look at them. Spread them like spokes. Covered in blood. For a long time I wash them in water from the pump in my parents' kitchen. Mouth wide open to let my scream escape.

Two of them have joined forces to question Maureen, who has always refused to see them, alleging she was ill. Now this morning they are here, sitting across from Maureen in her bottle-green kitchen. Maureen's bulging eyes go from McKenna to Richard. Then to the two men's hats on the table, finally resting on the Old Chum calendar up on the wall. Her ivory-colored face turns pink occasionally, is covered with sweat. She makes no attempt to wipe her face but stands, arms at her sides, as if it was her own idea to be exhibited in public with the hot flushes of her ripe age, sweating and deeply offended. "You're too old for me," Stevens told her on the night of August 31. August 31, August 31, she repeats, time having stopped in her mind on that date precisely. Her entire life settled on the night of . . . Nora and Olivia's youth, radiant and intact, is set down for a moment across from Maureen to scoff at her, before . . . Whatever is done, whatever is said, they will always be fifteen and seventeen years old. Might as well reconcile herself to it and consider time to be closed forever. Pretend to address the calendar on the wall, while the two policemen keep asking the same questions. The Old Chum fellows are reassuring in a different way than the policemen. Flat on the paper there, with no depth or real life, they maintain their poses and smile endlessly. The fellow in red, the fellow in green. Their buttoned cardigans. Their English look. Their long pipes. A cloud of smoke. Old Chum in huge letters. She keeps turning over what everyone knows. The time the two cousins arrived. The time they left. Then she stops, out of breath. All speech is cut off in her at the roots, where there is nothing but danger, rumors, and confusion. McKenna pushes her a little further into this forbid-

den zone, seems to want to shine a harsh light into her very
heart. She lowers her head. Starts staring at the tips of her
new shoes. Can't help thinking how pretty they are, with their
narrow straps. Yes, yes, yes, she wasn't in bed yet when Nora's
father, beside himself, came and knocked at her door around
half-past eleven on the night of August 31. Couldn't sleep.
Too tired and nervous. Looked at the moonlight through
the window in the upstairs bedroom. Saw a man going up
the path from the beach to the road. Didn't recognize him . . .

"But wasn't the moon very bright?"

"Didn't recognize him, didn't . . ."

She repeats without raising her head, her new shoes no
longer finding favor in her eyes, while the floor covered with
knots moves beneath her feet, as if lifted by waves. She clutches
the table to keep from falling. Harping like an old woman:
didn't recognize him, didn't recognize him. Shudders from
head to foot. Says she's sick.

"What time was it when you saw the man climbing up the
path from the beach?"

Once again the calendar on the wall with the two Old Chum
fellows. Their reassuring steadiness. Sees nothing but them.
While at her feet the world moves and trembles. One specific
hour out of all the rest keeps pounding inside Maureen's
head. There's no danger in mentioning that hour aloud because she didn't recognize the man who . . . Might as well
answer them once and for all, calm them down, in a way,
with a straightforward statement. Her voice detached and
clear.

"Ten to eleven. It was ten to eleven by my Big Ben clock
when I saw the man climb up the path onto the road."

When the wind stops altogether. A rare occurrence. Catches its breath for a moment. Plays dead. The sun stops too. All life in suspense. The breathing of the air becomes visible, quivering gently. I saw it. I, Percival, son of John and Bea Brown. Saw it with my own eyes. Saw the day breathe. The first time, I hadn't been born yet. Saw it through my mother's navel, as if it were a little window. The second time it was yesterday on the shore. Such silence suddenly. Even the gulls gripped by the incomprehensible silence. The air's pure breath. No wind. The silent waves rock my brother Stevens's flatboat, which is tied to a post in the sand. Before the wild gusts of wind start up again, and the murmuring waves, I noticed an object shining on the sand. The blue object probably took advantage of the absence of wind and the arrest of all things to alight there, in the sand. The wave returns, bathing it and making it even bluer. It is drying in the sun. Is covered with water once more. Is subjected to the back-and-forth motion of the wave. I pick it up cautiously, like a live shiny fish. A round object, a blue bracelet, come from the depths of the sea.

Took the bracelet back to the house. It passes from hand to hand. Each hand seems reluctant to give it up. The blue bracelet transfixed in the hollows of palms. Is turned over and over, cautiously. Like an unlucky object. No words exchanged. Only gestures. The bracelet passes from one to the next. Becomes more and more unlucky. Burdened with evil spells. The absence of speech is all the more troubling because all our thoughts, already ripe and fluttering about the room, resemble moths around a lamp. I hear my mother's and my father's thoughts, so loud that I begin to cry. Stevens's silence.

Haven't seen the blue bracelet again.

After the bracelet, the belt. The sea is vast, its waves go everywhere, on the shore, into crevices. The tide washed the belt onto a foreign shore. Strangers picked it up. At Cap Sec. Strangers phoned the general store in Griffin Creek. To advise the people of Griffin Creek. When the strangers called I was there with my father. I looking at the candies through the glass, he examining a black leather halter lined in red felt that hung on the wall among the harnesses and whips. The smell of new leather. The telephone on the wall beside the harness. In the smell of leather. Started to ring. My father's abrupt move. He picks it up as if he were at home. Listens. Says nothing. Hangs up. Walks out of the store like a madman. Orders me to follow him. My father's old Ford like an unpolished black box, dull, the color of a hearse. Its broad channeled gray running boards. My father and I in the car bouncing over the stones on the road. Pick up Stevens. The dust is blinding us. They left me in the car at Cap Sec. My father and Stevens don't take the time to open the wooden gate. Broke it. By kicking. Rushed at it. Emerge from a strange house. You can clearly see the pink belt, the end with a metal buckle, sticking out of my father's pocket. Back at the house my father throws the belt in the stove where supper is cooking. A scorched smell fills the kitchen as I eat my pea soup. I think about Nora's pink dress. But I won't tell anyone, or they'll whip me.

Green ferns and green childhood will never return. Nora and Olivia are lost. Today I rolled in the rusty autumn ferns. The russet odor is too strong, it chokes me. The Atkins girls' green smell is finished. They suddenly grew too big. Real women, with woman's blood flowing between their thighs every month. Stevens told me that. They should have stayed small, like before. Played together making bread on the shore. Fished for tadpoles in the rock pools. Everything that happened is the fault of childhood past. Let everything be as it was before. Olivia, Nora, and I together on the shore. Their smell. Fern, fern, I love young green ferns, the fiddleheads we eat with butter and salt in the summer. Rolling in the russet autumn ferns. Alone. All alone.

If anything else is to come, it will come from the sea.

Each wave examined by me. Search out their secrets hidden in the foam. Every wave felt as it tenses and swells. Every wave blown by me when it spreads on the sand and dies. The residue of each wave spied on, watched. Its white froth, its pebbles, gray or veined in rose, its pale sea grasses in wet bouquets, its gleaming seaweed, its agates, its bit of wood and blue glass. Lacework of debris on the sand. At low tide the people of Griffin Creek walk on the sandbar. Heads down. Seemingly searching for agates. Their footprints, as soon as they're formed, are erased by the underground water seeping through the soft sand. Human monsters have been here, dressed in rubber, masks and tubes. Exploring the bottom of the sea. Dredge underwater like heavy formless fish. By examining the sand of the bay so much they drive out all the marine creatures sleeping on a bed of sand, make them rise to the surface amid seething bubbles. If it's true that my cousins now live among the fish, the rubber men will bring them up from their muddy holes, will bring them onto the shore, crowned with seaweed, all white, with their eyes wide open.

The coat! I wasn't the one who found it. Or my father. Or Stevens. It was Nora's father, walking two paces ahead of me on the shore, head bent, gazing down at the wet sand. The coat limp, rolled up like a rag. Its finish all gone. In a heap on the sand. So wet it looks black. Immediately thought of Olivia. Of Olivia's black coat. Everybody thought of Olivia. As it dries we can see that it's not black but brown. Nora's coat, her father says. Powdered with sand and with salt, with grasses and shells. Nora's coat ruined, damaged, lost. And Nora, Nora, Nora, who is russet and gay. Nora, her mother and father repeat. While the coat is spread on the kitchen table. McKenna promptly wraps the coat in gray paper. Exhibit, he says, rolling his pointed little eyes to the back of their sockets.

The policemen watch us without respite. Our speech, our silence, our slightest gesture, even our immobility and our very sleep are gone over with a fine-toothed comb. The person who betrays us will push all of us into dishonor.

At Cap Sauvagine, the Jeremy Lords confirmed Bob Allen's visit on the evening of August 31. Couldn't say exactly when he came or when he left.

The autumn trees are at their finest. Gold, bronze, and flame in wild bouquets against the harsh blue sky. Though it's still daylight, Maureen has pulled the shades at all her windows. It's odd to see blind windows, milky green. There are small holes of different shapes in Maureen's shades where the sun seeps in. Little dots of sun, tiny rents of sun dance on the quilt. And on Maureen's brow, making her bring her hand to her eyes. Then she turns to face the wall. It seems now that spangles of light are stinging her back like fire. Maureen pulls the cover over her head. Safely ensconced in her bed, she says over and over, half-stifled, "My God, my God."

Downstairs, someone knocks at the door, shakes the door, pounds with all his might. Yelling: "Mrs. MacDonald! Mrs. MacDonald!"

Her narrow feet in felt slippers. She pulls her coat over her nightgown. While downstairs the pounding and shouting continue.

Maureen apologizes for not being dressed at eleven o'clock in the morning. Says she's sick. McKenna shows his ugly teeth, says he likes catching people as they really are. Taking off neither his hat nor his coat he straddles a chair. Flicks his hat to the back of his head.

Lost in the coat, which is too big for her, Maureen frees one pale hand, with difficulty raises her arm, and with her fingertips grazes her heavy, dark, white-threaded hair.

"Why, after spending the whole summer with you, did Stevens leave on the night of August 31?"

"The summer chores were done. I didn't need a hired man. He wanted to see his parents before he went back to Florida."

"Did you see Stevens the night of August 31?"

"Yes, around half-past seven. Stevens and Bob Allen were with the girls when they arrived here."

"Did you see him again later that night?"

"Yes, during the investigation. When Nora's father came here with one of Olivia's brothers."

"What time was it?"

"Eleven-thirty, I think."

"How did he look?"

"Same as usual."

The east wind has blown for three days and nights. You can hear the roar of the sea through the closed houses. Comes in through keyholes, through the cracks between boards, the hollows of chimneys. Hands over my ears, I still can hear the sea's hoarse breathing. Its salty breath on my face. The wind has devoured the sun. No more morning sun coming up on the horizon, at the source of the sun. The wind smothers the sun and it no longer puts in an appearance. A violet glow replaces the sun. You can see as though it were the middle of day. But everyone knows it's not the sun. Too dark. Lightning-colored. Not lightning that zigzags through the sky. But a glimmer of violet lightning spread out all around, over sea and sky. The trees moan, bend, then straighten up. Branches break, are carried away by the wind. Eddies of leaves cross the road opposite our house. The tousled, cracking trees are stripped of summer, assume their winter shapes, pure and bare. Sometimes torrents of rain fall on houses, woods, and fields, joining the water of the sea, in eager, sizzling drops. Then everything dries in the violet air, in the dry wind. No fishermen venture out to sea now. Stevens had to put his flat away in the boathouse. At the end of the third day the east wind lay down at our door, growling like a dog. My father decided to go and dig clams, for the sea was still too rough for fishing. With my heavy red sweater on top of my overalls, my rubber boots, my knife at my belt like Stevens, carrying a bucket, I go out with my father to dig for clams.

We can see that the shore has been stirred up and turned over like a plowed field, in total disorder. Debris of all sorts—whole logs, bits of wood, garlands of kelp, green, yellow, or red, a rusty teakettle, a twisted bicycle wheel. With my knife

I scrape off clams that cling to the muddy rocks. I'm in water to my knees. Around thirty feet ahead of me, my father has stopped. He's attentively examining the bottom of the water.

More stooped than ever, his hair sticking stiffly out of his head, he looks like a kingfisher, fascinated by his underwater prey. My father turns around and calls me. I advance toward my father, feeling the water's resistance at every step. My boots are leaden, my knees feel as if they won't bend. Soon the icy water is over the tops of my boots, seeping inside my boots, wetting my knees and thighs. I look at what my father's looking at. Don't understand what it is that we see in the icy water, my father and I. I see but I don't understand. Don't want to understand. Only look. A calamity has occurred in Griffin Creek, and we're looking at that calamity under the water, my father and I, refusing to understand. My father moves first one leg, then the other. Says he's cold, says we must hurry before the tide rises. I say: "A dead body?" My father says: "Help me." Big leaden clouds move across the sky. And still that violet glow all over, covering the sky and the sea. Beams pierce the water's surface. Make points of light on the poor carcass, without arms or legs, lying there at our feet in three feet of water. A thing with no name. Can't have one. Unnamcable. Even if my uncle Ben maintains that it's his daughter Nora. No, it's not true. Impossible to understand and name. Haven't had time yet. Only saw with my eyes. The image hasn't yet entered my brain. Has no name. Can't have one. Her torn pink dress. Useless to call Nora. To maintain as my uncle Ben does that it's Nora. It comes from the sea, from the very depths of the sea and the fish have half-devoured it.

John Erwin McKenna was a detective in Montreal for four-
teen years. He became a building contractor. Chief Leroux
from Quebec City sent for him specially to question the inhabitants of Griffin Creek. On the pretext that he's English-
speaking and more adept than a Catholic priest at hearing
confessions. Since the discovery of Nora's body, Stevens and
Bob Allen are questioned several times a day. They're the
only ones the police seem interested in now.

He enters without knocking. Shouts: "Everybody out! I want to talk to Stevens!" My father and mother go out without locking the door. I hide in the woodshed under the stairs. McKenna undresses. Coat, hat, and jacket are tossed in a heap on the chair. He seems in high spirits, as if he's getting ready to tell a good joke. In shirtsleeves, with red-and-blue elastics to hold up the sleeves which are too long, his vest unbuttoned, he inspects the place. While Stevens, motionless, close to the table, watches him come and go. There's a slit in the door to the woodshed. I have a good view of the preparations made by McKenna and my brother, who doesn't move. By nosing about everywhere, McKenna finally discovered the little room out on the gallery, with no cellar and no electricity. McKenna rubs his hands. Tells Stevens to follow him. Lights an old kerosene lamp that's out there, with its chimney. Rubs his hands again. Puts on his jacket because it's cold in the little room, which is used as a junk closet. Now Stevens enters the room. McKenna shuts the door. I see no one now. Hear them whisper. No distinct words. Stevens's low, obstinate voice. A lesson well learned, tiresome to repeat. McKenna's voice bright and animated, bursts in at regular intervals, loud and clear, in a joyous refrain.

"Come on now, tell me everything."

I also hear,

"You'll feel better afterwards."

Nothing more has happened for a while now. Not a sound. Or a breath. Or breathable air. The silence persists behind the door where my brother Stevens and McKenna are shut in. Such a long private conversation. A clinch, rather. I'm sure they're fighting in the dense silence. Someone's life is at stake. Breathing in one another's face. Exhausting one another like maniacal wrestlers. The same evil perspiration sweated by McKenna and my brother. The smell of an animal's den seeps under the door. Comes to me in my hiding place. Ah! All this attention exhausts me. I've got no strength left. Want to sleep.

A little nap curled up among the logs. Then I open the woodshed door a crack. To breathe and stretch my legs. There's hardly any wood in the woodshed. Bits of bark, splinters, sawdust. The smell of wood makes you sneeze. I hear footsteps in the little room. Curl up in my hiding place. Afraid of slivers. My brother Stevens opens the door. Leans on the doorpost. Starts to walk in the kitchen. Laboriously. As if he were following his footprints as he walks. Wondering each time which foot to set down on the floor. He doesn't look like my brother Stevens. No expression. Or pride. Features drawn. Arms and legs too long. Looking lost. He drinks from the kitchen pump. Puts his face under the water. Pumps with all his might. Then stands up again. Wipes his face, neck, and hair with his handkerchief. McKenna's powerful voice calls out from the next room.

"Come back here. I've still got a few little details to ask you."

My brother Stevens turns around in the room, looking like a dog being pulled by its leash and having trouble bringing itself to obey. McKenna's voice turns pleading, soft, almost tender.

"You understand, it's essential that we clear this up. That's what I'm here for."

He says again, reassuring and jovial,

"You'll feel better after."

The door shuts again on Stevens and McKenna. Stevens's voice more and more distant. A sort of monotonous, endless murmur that McKenna no longer interrupts. Suddenly the taut thread of Stevens's voice breaks. Silence fills the room once more. McKenna plays dead behind the door. The whole house plays dead along with McKenna. Walls, boards, beams, doors and windows, furniture, curtains and I, aching all over in my storage room. The countryside all around seemingly dead, in reality as attentive as a cat lying in wait for a mouse. A little more and my brother Stevens's secret will escape him and scamper around us, on little mouse feet, in the unbearable silence. I must warn him right away, before it's too late. I emerge from my hiding place. Push open the door of the little room. The smells of Stevens and McKenna mixed together rise to my face. I stand there, planted on my two feet. McKenna takes a little bottle from his pocket. My brother Stevens shakes his head. His neck broken. His head drooping onto his chest. On the table, a pale pencil drawing. Looks like a cadastral survey. The yellow pencil has a red eraser at the end. The lamp chimney is black with soot.

"Be a man. Don't worry."

McKenna puts on his jacket. Pockets the drawing. Pushes me away from the door. A moment later we hear the motor of his car starting up like a whirlwind.

There's some snow now in the hollows of the rocks. And strangers all over the shore. On a fine November morning, cold and filled with echoes. Squeezed into their winter coats they carry picks and shovels. Dig holes in the sand. Pass from hand to hand the map that Stevens drew. They seem to be playing "run sheep run." Have only one idea in their heads. To catch out my brother Stevens. Throw him kicking and screaming into one of those big gray canvas bags they're dragging along the beach to put in the pieces of evidence, they say.

Before leaving, they pushed back the sea like a rug that's rolled to the horizon. They took my brother Stevens away in a big shiny black car. Someone says that Jack McKenna's already pocketed two hundred and fifty dollars, or half of the promised reward for the capture of Stevens. Wet sand before me, as far as the eye can see. Rocks, wet or dry, form pointed bumps here and there on the sandbar. I must blink very hard to see the sea in the distance, a thin liquid line along the rim of the sky. Someone says my brother Stevens is in jail in a city of asphalt and brick. Very far away. Farther than the sandbar. Farther even than the liquid horizon. The coroner's inquest. The clicking typewriter. I clearly see McKenna's pointed yellow shoe kicking my brother Stevens on the leg. To make him say he's a murderer. The sound of the typewriter swallows my brother's words as he utters them. It's as if he were saying nothing at all. Too much noise. McKenna claims that he can hear. I know he's lying. Stevens's words run into the sea. They'll never be fished out of the roaring water. A great flat expanse the gray color of oysters. Beyond the sea and the ocean. Florida. Orange trees in blossom. Snakes. Knives. My brother whose skinny hands clutch a prison's bars. And Olivia who hasn't come back to Griffin Creek. Since the evening of August 31. Hasn't been cast up by the tide, like Nora, onto the shore of Griffin Creek. Hasn't been enjoined by her father and brothers to come out of her carcass and say, "Here I am, it's me, Olivia." She has taken the ocean road. Has become a pure spirit of water, haze and mist upon the sea. Nora has not come back to Griffin Creek any more than Olivia. Even though her father and mother have identified her and called her by name. Addressing something nameless that wasn't Nora. Could not be Nora, alive and gay, ablaze in the sun. None has the power to summon the dead and make them surge out of their bones. Nora has not come back to Griffin Creek any more than Olivia. Even though they claim that Nora's buried in the little graveyard that overlooks the sea. My two cousins are lost at the bottom of the ocean. Neither father nor mother nor brothers will ever haul them out. I exhaust myself looking for the line that divides the waters. Never have I seen the tide so low. Perhaps the tide will never return again to the land of Griffin Creek, in growling, singing waves. For a moment I see once more the nearly invisible strand of shimmering water. Silver highlights leap in the distance like glistening fish. My cousins glisten like silvery fish. Spring in the blue air, burst in silvery bubbles. Their peals of laughter leap up to the sky in frail drops, touch the sun, then sputter like water on flames. Never have I seen the tide so low. The ocean so far. Too much wind.

OLIVIA OF THE HIGH SEA

(no date)

*Your heart will break and you
will become foam upon the sea.*

Hans Christian Andersen

SOMEONE HAS CERTAINLY killed me. Then slipped away. On tiptoe.

The sweetbriar hedges have lost their perfume. Maureen's garden has been overrun by weeds, yet white roses live on against the fence, deteriorated, odorless. The gnarled black apple trees are now completely dead. The minister's garden smells of garlic and leeks. The forest comes closer and closer to the scattered frame houses that stand in fallow fields where fireweed abounds. My powerful shellfish odor penetrates everywhere. At will, I haunt the nearly deserted village, with its closed windows. Transparent and fluid as a watery sigh, without flesh or soul, reduced to mere desire, I visit Griffin Creek day after day, night after night. In gusts of wind, of spindrift, I pass between the ill-sealed planks of walls, the cracks of worm-eaten windows, I cross the motionless bedroom air like an adverse wind, stirring up imperceptible eddies in the closed rooms, chilly corridors, rickety stairways, half-rotted galleries, devastated gardens. In vain do I whistle at keyholes, slip under beds stripped of blankets and mattresses, blow fine dust, puff out the faded cretonne flounce on the cosy corner in my cousin Maureen's little sitting room, inch my way, dripping wet, into uncle Nicholas's daydreams, tangle the blonde braids of my uncle's servant girls: the one I am seeking is no longer there.

For oh: life's clock has just now stopped, and I am no longer of this world. Something has happened in Griffin Creek. Time stopped for good on the night of August 31, 1936.

In the small closed sitting room that smells like a cellar, the unchanging time is posted on the gilt face of cousin Maureen's clock. Amid the profusion of crocheted doilies and tiny knickknacks, the echo of the half hour after nine lingers in the rarefied air like a dream. Half-past nine. I can turn back the time only that far. Scarcely further. Only until . . . My bones dissolved in the sea like salt. It is half-past nine in the evening, August 31, 1936.

I am seventeen years old, and my cousin Nora is fifteen. My cousin Maureen is ageless, though for some time now mysterious waves have been passing over her smooth widow's face. Pallor, sudden flushes, fluttering eyelids, untimely smiles, so many signs of a new and secret life.

My memory resembles those long garlands of seaweed that continue to grow on the surface of the sea after they've been cut. I can't stop hearing the sound of half-past nine. A solemn chiming fills my cousin Maureen's frame house. That clock her only treasure, I think, till he appeared, my cousin Stevens, standing in the doorway. No, no, it's not Maureen he looks at through the screen. He's looking at me, and it's a different day, in my father's house. I'm ironing shirts, enveloped in hot steam.

Why not confine myself to the bottle-green plank walls of Maureen's kitchen? The knots bulging under the shiny paint. Nothing has happened yet, and I'm alive. Focus on the portrait of King George V stuck up with four gilt thumbtacks. His royal beard carefully trimmed. Across from him, on the other wall, the two fellows on the Old Chum calendar smoke never-ending pipes. Eternity is like that, poor chromolithographs fastened to the wall. As long as memory's smooth surface still endures. The tick-tock of the clock in the room next door. The peal of Nora's laughter. Maureen's muffled voice. I who never finish a sentence. Too pressed for time by the urgency of life. The warm fudge melts in our mouths. We have just enough time before half-past nine sounds. Promised aunt Alice to come home early.

Suddenly Maureen is talking too loud, over Nora's and my heads. Not seeing us, it seems. As if she were touching something hidden far away in the countryside. As soon as we're gone I'm sure Maureen's ears and head will fill with the regular, monotonous sound of her superb clock, she'll listen to it like a living heart, noticing only the passage of time, like someone waiting intensely for an improbable grace. And what difference can it make to me if my cousin Maureen is expecting someone or not? No, no, it's not Stevens. Just her hired man. For the summer. The summer only. Anyway, my cousin's at least fifty. Lord, is it possible that summer's over already? Already August 31 and nothing's happened. Oh yes, aunt Irene's death, Stevens's arrival. No, no, it's not that. I mean that nothing's happened to me in particular. I turned seventeen on June 13 and nothing particular has happened to me. The night of the barn dance, Stevens danced with me. The warmth of his body close to mine, his smell of tobacco and alcohol. His beady eyes in the shadow of his hat. One morning he took me in his arms as I was coming out of the water, streaming wet, for a moment only, until my brother Patrick arrived. I struggled in the sun and water like an eel in his hands. I'm strong and I won't be pushed around that easily. One day, my love, we will struggle on the shore in the light of the moon that enchants and maddens. Without grace or mercy. Until one of us touches the sand with both shoulders, for the count of one minute. Lord, I said "my love," without thinking, as if I were singing. No, no, it's not true. I'm dreaming. That man is evil. He wants nothing so much as to awaken the deepest dread within me and revel in it, as in something marvelous. The oldest, deepest dread that is no longer completely mine, but that of my mother pregnant with me, and of my grandmother who . . .

Giggling with my cousin Nora. Big chunks of dark fudge smeared over our teeth and tongues. It's fun to visit people. Maureen is staring at both of us, her big sea-green eyes scandalized in their sockets. At times Maureen laughs with us. But her eyes don't move (they keep watching us), don't crease with laughter, they retain their wild, scandalized expression.

"Well, girls, how old are you now?"

Our clear, precise answers, our youth, ring out in the shiny bottle-green kitchen, mingling with the smell of chocolate. Maureen lowers her gaze, looks closely at her faded hands flat on her knees.

Nora says the summer sun has spotted her face with freckles and it's time that it stopped. She laughs. Her sparkling teeth. Her pointed little chin. Her hot fudge breath. The clock rings out in the next room, with great ceremony. The wooden house seems too modest for such sumptuous chiming. Maureen says all her savings went into it. She gets up, her whole body sensing the urgency of passing time. She shows us to the front door as if we were important visitors. On the way, we brush against lace doilies and are amazed at their profusion, endlessly repeated on every piece of furniture. The clock's pendulum swings from left to right, from right to left. Nora says there are two pieces of fudge left on the blue plate on the kitchen table.

"Just enough for your hired man when he comes in, Maureen."

Nora's laughter has already left Maureen's little sitting room. It ripples, light and crystalline, through the nighttime landscape bathed in moonlight. From her doorstep Maureen waves to us.

"Bye-bye, girls, bye-bye."

The lunar night closes in around us. I hear my cousin Maureen in the distance warning us about running into the wrong sort of people.

The sea shimmers, each small wave like so many little mirrors tossing gently under the moon. It's only the attraction of the sea, my heart, only the fascination of the moon. Nora and I should run, hurry home, before there appears in our path one particular face, come into the world to ruin us, both of us, in the shiny night, himself bathed in savage light, the cold white light of the moon radiant on his face, his very eyes seemingly made of that luminous icy matter.

I have nothing more to do here. Time has stopped throughout the length and breadth of this taiga land. Let us leave behind there the survivors of a vanished time, uncle Nicholas and his sleeping servant girls. Let us regain the high sea. Light as a bubble, salt sea foam, quicker than thought, more nimble than dream, I leave the seashore of my childhood and the obscure memories of my former life. Like a sea bird gently rocking between two waves, I look out at the expanse of water as far as the eye can see, swelling, distended, like a woman's womb under the thrust of its fruit. A whole mass, dense and deep, ferments and rises down below, while the wave forms on the surface, scarcely a fold, then a wall of water rising, climbing, reaching its apogee, very high, then rearing up, booming, bursting, throwing itself on the shore and subsiding in a fringe of snowy foam on the gray sand of Griffin Creek.

The sand streams through her fingers. She has the hands of a precious living child. She's a child made for life, from the tips of her nails to the roots of her hair. She might be three or four years old. She builds sand castles on the shore of Griffin Creek. A fringe of blonde hair falls into her eyes. The wet granular sand clings to her fingers. She carefully wipes her palms on the blue cotton shirt that serves as her dress. Suddenly he is there behind her. His slight shadow right above. Like the shadow of a cloud. She need only lift her eyes to him. Her bare feet, her skinned knees, her hair sticking out of her head in straight tufts. The little girl blinks, takes a long look at the little boy, from his feet to his head, luminous and golden, suffused with pale light, his head half lost in the wind and sky like a pale disheveled sun, she thinks, she who has already seen the row of sunflowers against the chicken coop turning white in the sun, in the dazzle of mid-day.

Now he is crouching in the sand beside her. Looks closely at the sand castles. Looks closely at the little girl. Doesn't know which he admires more, the sand heaped up in tidy rows or the little girl herself, who has built it all. She is breathing against his shoulder, hiding behind her bangs. With his fingertips he grazes the little girl's cheek. The little girl's cheek is cool as a shadow. The little boy's fingers blaze like the sun. Who will be the first to shout with joy in the wind, amid the clamor of the sea birds?

"Stevens! Olivia!" says one of the mothers over there, who knits on her folding stool.

The little boy zigzags across the sand, his bare feet striving to follow the black border of seaweed left by the last tide.

A man at the top of the cliff whistles very loud between his fingers, calling the little boy. Without raising his head the little boy keeps walking on the seaweed. The man whistles louder and louder. His long arched silhouette stands out in black against the sky. Now he is waving his arms. The little boy persists in following the line of the seaweed along the sand. He must be warned immediately, before the storm gathers up above and starts hurtling down the hill in a cloud of pebbles and sand. The little girl cries out to warn the little boy. Someone says that the boy is unmanageable and must be taken in hand.

"Stevens! Olivia!" repeats one of the mothers standing on the sand, holding her knitting. John Brown has caught up with his son, seized him by the throat. He shakes him like a tree in a storm. In the distance the boathouse, its blind side, windowless, all gray planks.

Too many old images, colors, sounds . . . He whistled for him, like a dog. No, I won't tolerate it. Let us leave this shore. Let memories disappear in the sand with the speed of crabs digging their holes. Let the high sea come, a gray thread between gray sandbar and gray sky. Flee. Rejoin the tide as it draws back to the deep water's highest point. The open sea. Its harsh breathing. Slip along the horizon. Embrace the wind, glide upon the smooth slopes of the wind, soar like an invisible gull. Quiver upon the sea like a tiny speck of light. My heart transparent on the sea. Pure spirit of water, my body left behind on sandbanks and masses of salt, a thousand blind fish have gnawed at my bones. Someone has certainly . . . Cast me still alive into the calm lunar depths of that deep bay, between Cap Sec and Cap Sauvagine.

His hot fingers on my cheek in the summer sun. He, a pale tousled sun. Can only cry out. Like Percival. With the wild birds in the sky. With joy. Soon with sorrow and dread when John Brown seizes his son by the throat.

My mother drops her knitting on the sand, takes me in her arms and gently consoles me.

I like to kiss my mother's neck, taste her white skin and her odor of green apples. My big brothers prowl around us, snickering and calling me a baby. My father has asked my mother not to kiss her sons any more because they're too big now and she might turn them into sissies. For a long time now my brothers have been putting steel tips on their boots. They talk loud. Swear as soon as they think they're alone.

Why is my mother so sad? She always seems to be looking straight ahead of her at invisible, terrible things. I would like to console her, heal the pain that is gnawing away at her. Her gentle face, withered too soon, by what sorrow, what secret transgression, to revive her at once, return to her her murdered youth. Perhaps my brothers make too much noise as they walk through the house, clicking their heels? Perhaps they swear too loud? Or is it my father's heavy tread that resounds too noisily in the silent rooms? I saw a bloodstain on the sheet in my mother's big bed. What sort of wound is it, God? Who has wounded my mother? I shall take my mother with me, take her far away. To the bottom of the sea perhaps, where there are palaces of shells, strange flowers, many-colored fish, streets where you breathe the water calmly, like air. We shall live together silently, effortlessly.

My mother died one night when we were all awake around her bed. I saw the shadow of death pass over my mother's face like the shadow of a cloud coming from the farthest part of her, passing from the tips of her toes all along her body, under the sheets, then reaching her face and getting lost in her hair, on the pillow. This was done very quickly and lightly, like a somber wind, weightless, scarcely more than a whisper. Now she is gone forever. A rapid substitution, quick as the wind, and my mother's body was no longer on the bed. In its place, beneath the sheets, a sort of recumbent statue, quite flat, scarcely marking the tightly drawn sheets. On the white pillow they had placed a small face made of chilly ivory. Only the wreath of hair like an unkempt nest was still alive.

Two days earlier, when the potatoes were being dug. Lying in my little bed, beside my mother's, I forget her warning to close my eyes when she is undressing. I see blue marks on her arms and shoulders. She is breathing fast and seems tired.

"I'll rest tomorrow when the potatoes are done."

The next day I follow her into the field to help her pull up as many potatoes as possible so she can rest as soon as possible. The sound of her breathing, furrow after furrow. The earth black and stiff. Powdery snow in the hollows. The wind. I blow on my fingers to warm them. My mother, who is sparing with words as if the passage of words through her lips exhausts her, says it's madness for snow to be falling in October, a hardship for poor people.

Before she changed into a statue under the sheets, my mother made me swear to be obedient and to take care of the house. My father and brothers, she counseled to watch out for the little girl. We all promise. Then, not another word from her. Only the hoarse whistle of her breathing and her life that is running out in her chest.

Now who will watch out for me, spy on me rather, and constantly bother me? No, not my father. It seems as if my father sees nothing and hears nothing. He's all taken up with his mental calculations of the price of milk and potatoes. Dreaming of a miraculous catch of fish. My brothers are at the age when they despise girls. Avoid talking to me and looking at me. Merely stand on guard around me, keeping me a prisoner in the house.

My cousin Stevens probably shares my brothers' opinion about girls. He doesn't recognize me now that he's grown up. Boys are a rare species, or so they think, and needn't lower themselves by associating with girls. I like to watch them play baseball, slamming the ball with such force, throwing down the bat, taking off as fast as their legs can carry them. Their shouting. The noise of their running, the dull thud of the ball on the bat. The ground is worn down by their boys' games, the grass pulled up in clumps, the sand turned over in little yellow clods. Nora, Percival, and I watch them slamming the ball and running like lunatics. We try to shout as loud as they do, to encourage them.

Impossible to leave Griffin Creek for the moment. Flat calm

on the sand as far as the eye can see. The sea has drawn back. I wait for the tide to rise and for the favorable wind to carry me out to the high sea. Transparent and shallow, having crossed through the pass of death, dependent henceforth on the winds and the tides, I remain on the shore like a living person waiting for a train.

I look at a little girl who sits motionless on the sand, her knees to her chin, arms encircling her knees. She is there in the thud of the rising sea, at the limit of our attention. Peering into the mystery of the water. All her body is aware of the water's murmur, heading for her. Wave after wave, she questions the water so as to draw out its secret. Is this fringe of foam at her feet her mother's dress? Is it possible that her mother's unfastened dress is rustling like this at her feet, coming to lick at her feet with a hundred cold little tongues? If I look carefully, along with the little girl, not blinking, through the depths of the nascent wave, if I join the little girl and call out with all the strength in my speechless being, concentrated like a rock, I shall enter everything at once. The mystery of my mother's life and death will have no more secrets from me. Perhaps I shall even see her face in the water's mirror and its stormy sound.

Still, at the very moment when the little girl is about to grasp and know everything, her mother's face forming in the salt, one feature, one marvel at a time, the water darkens, a boy's voice and then two call from the top of the cliff.

"Olivia! Olivia! What are you doing? You must go home!"

They called me Olivia. From the top of the cliff my brothers shout themselves hoarse calling out my name. Shall I leap at the sound of my name, inhabit my name anew, dress myself in it as in a light garment? Olivia, Olivia, call out Sidney and Patrick. I would only have to climb up the path, go where I'm being called, to cook and keep the house clean. That's my story, waiting up there for me with my father and my brothers, my frame house with its covered gallery. It would be enough to return to my name as to an empty shell. Pick up the thread of my life. Time stopped in Griffin Creek. The

night of August 31, 1936. You need only look at the time
fastened there on the wall of my cousin Maureen's little sitting
room. Half-past nine on that night.

The door is wide open on the moon-white night. Nora and
I cross over the threshold, disappear into the night. Topple
over the edge. Forever. All the rest is only the effect of the
moon on the sea, of a great lunar fury on the deserted shore.

In vain do they call me Olivia in their dreams. Probably my
uncle Nicholas, who's a minister. Or perhaps even the one
who . . . Has already left Griffin Creek long ago, has taken
refuge in the war, urged on by the military authorities on
the other side of the ocean. And if he were to call me, as he
is today, wherever he may be, am I not absent from my name,
from my flesh and bones, limpid as a tear upon the sea?

From waiting so long for the rising tide to disappear on the
horizon, I foam the coastline of Griffin Creek with all of its
outmoded images.

The little girl grew very fast. Here she is in the boys' arena,
invited there by them to share their games on the bare grass.
Once only. Her skinned knees, her long legs, her short skirt,
the speed of her running, the precise way she moves. The
little girl runs in the field, scores. Like a big pair of scissors,
Stevens thinks. Game over. He approaches her. Sweats his
strong boy's smell in the summer heat. She just smells like a
girl, streaming wet from her run. Who will be the first to
breathe deep of the other, eyes shut in pleasure? Not yet a
man, not yet hidden under his brown felt hat, his pale eyes
exposed, Stevens examines Olivia with astonishment before
catching up, with long strides, with the group of boys who
are growing impatient.

The little girl leans against the fence. Shuts her eyes. No,
no, it's not the first time. At what age do these things start?
Joy, with all its savor, at one stroke. To exist in such joy at
Griffin Creek, on the edge of a baseball diamond where grass,
trees, clamoring, light, water, and the nearby sand, the birds

that pass over our heads, crying out, all exist along with us, in a single breath.

The boy was absent from Griffin Creek for five years. He became a man far away from us, fulfilling his transformation into a man apart from us, like a snake that hides to change its skin. He bought boots and a brown felt hat. His shoulders roll when he walks and his eyes are the color of blue ash. Here he is now, flattened against the kitchen screen door.

O memory, reform this heart as liquid as green water, find its precise place between my ribs, reform the white hip, place violet flowers in the hollow sockets of my eyes, let my redis-covered person appear on the sea as I walk across the water, very fast, toward Griffin Creek, straight to my father's land before summer ends. Resume my place in the kitchen before the appearance of . . . He has only to climb up the path and cross the road. The house is there, slightly off to one side, massive and closed. Its gray planks the color of driftwood. It's easy to slip inside again, carried along by the gusts of wind, causing the frame of the roof to creak and rustling every living thing for several miles around. The oats lie down in the sun, rise up and billow like a green and shallow sea.

The little girl is ironing in the kitchen, her head bent in the hot steam from the irons, being careful not to pull any buttons off the white shirt. Her faded blue dress is too short, but good enough for working around the house. All around the tangled wind creeps under doorsills, its spellbinding song reaching to the heart of the ironing girl. I am she and she is I. I fit myself against her bones and her soul has no secrets from me. Her mass of blonde hair, her patient profile above the ironing board. Two irons are used. One that's passed back and forth along the damp cloth, the other heating up on the wood stove. Takes the iron's temperature by gently bringing it close to her cheek. As her mother and grand-mother did. The long line of gestures by the women of Griffin Creek bind her forever.

And the wind that swirls all around the house makes Griffin Creek ring out with the voices of patient women, ironers,

washerwomen, cooks, wives, pregnant, giving birth, mothers
of the living and the dead, desiring and desired in the bitter
wind.

She knew him at once as he stood in the door. His man's
stature. His man's voice. After five years' absence. Though
she pretended not to. Cling as long as possible to the precise
movements of the iron on damp cloth, a cohort of women
in the shadow of the wind begging her to go on ironing as
if nothing had happened.

I hear them say: Don't take your eyes off your ironing as
long as that bad boy's standing in the doorway. Out of a
thousand others. She looked him full in the face. Was looked
at full in the face by him. God, you mustn't, they all say in
the shadow of the wind, mothers and grandmothers on the
alert. While Olivia with her overheated iron scorches the cuff
of her brother Patrick's shirt.

He's like the tree planted in the middle of an earthly paradise.
The knowledge of good and evil have no secrets from him.
If only I wanted to I could learn it all from him, in one
stroke, life, death, everything. Never again would I be an
innocent simpleton silently ironing shirts. Only love could
turn me into a full-fledged woman, communicating as an
equal with my mother and grandmothers in the shadow of
the wind, using veiled terms, a knowing air, telling of the
mystery that ravages me body and soul.

His way of looming up behind my back when it's very windy
and you can't hear him coming. All of a sudden he's there.
Thinking he's hiding, the better to surprise me.

"Hi Olivia! Nice day, isn't it?"

He examines me from head to toe as I hang out the sheets
and the wind plasters my dress to my thighs. Am I to stop
all work and all movement, stand there motionless and be-
witched, both feet in the short grass behind my father's house,
caught in Stevens's gaze as in a net? My mother and grandmothers whisper to me in the fierce wind to do nothing about
it but concentrate on the wet sheets that feel so heavy in my

arms. He has already turned on his heel and gone to join Sidney and Patrick who are drinking beer on the gallery.

The great chalky women who lie in the little graveyard of Griffin Creek have nimble souls that have taken to the sea, changed into breath and mist. Among them, my mother, the coolest and the saltiest too, secretly speaks to me in my sweet native tongue and tells me to beware of Stevens.

All summer long, whenever I see him I tremble, as if my bones were knocking together inside me. Above all, he mustn't be aware of it. I must be straight and smooth in his presence. I think that very hard, while a burning flame ascends my neck, spreads over my cheeks and forehead. Above all, he mustn't be aware of it. If he saw me blush in his presence because he torments me, once, once only, I'd die of shame.

Let us leave this gray shore, return to the sea world, the twilight world of kelp, its broad forests and plains, the blue color, shading to black, of the great seas. Women's voices whistle amid the sea's foliage, rise up at times onto the ocean's expanse, a vast lament on the surface of the wind, only the cry of a dying whale is as harrowing. Certain sailors in the solitude of their watch, when night reigns over the sea, have heard these voices mingling with the clamor of the wind. They will never be the same, they pretend that they have dreamed and fear henceforth the black heart of the night. My equinoctial grandmothers, my high mother-tides and low, my smooth spells and my lulls, my seas of low water and of salt.

A certain distance seems necessary between me and Griffin Creek, between my earthly memories and my eternity as a sea anemone. Let the swell and the currents carry me beyond the horizon. Before disappearing, let that which serves as my eyes, not violet now and bathed in tears, or shining with delight and invisible, liquid, a drop of dew upon the immensity of the sea, let it linger on in Griffin Creek, let it see all the houses suddenly lit up in the night. A sign of celebration. All the houses have shining windows, orange, hot, reflected on the grass. Some nights are for being born, others for dying, but that one on the coast (one can already hear the music) is made for dancing in the smell of new-mown hay.

The fiddles creak and nothing can stop the accordion. A deep animal heat arises from everywhere at once, odorous and dense, panting little cries blend with the music. Men's shoes, women's shoes, some of them white with straps, face, come together, pursue, couple for a moment and then part. All these joyous pounding steps obey the master of the dance who calls out orders, hands cupped around his mouth. The ladies' chain, the men's, unfurl in good order, the figures are well drawn and the swinging is more and more rapid and breathless.

His long silhouette, motionless for a moment, standing in the doorway. Waves of night all around him. His white shirt. His face in the shadow of his hat. The shades of night project him into our midst with all the dazzle of his white shirt and his insolent life. The dance closes in around him, carries him along with us, stamping his feet and turning with us, breathing the same air, imbuing it with the odor of his sweat, in the sweltering heat of the barn. The dance alone is bearing me, rocking me, thinks Olivia, shutting her eyes, feeling the music in her very skin, while boys' hands graze her fingers, clasp her waist as she passes. It's Stevens who touched me, he has a little callus on his right hand. Don't look up. My mother and grandmothers counsel me very softly not to raise my eyes to him. Only the delight of dancing till morning in the odor of new-mown hay makes me turn my head, she thinks, only the delight of dancing possesses me and bewitches me. No, no, not Stevens. While faces and silhouettes light up now and then for a moment around her, in the swirling colors and smells. The minister's red hair, his massive shoulders leaning over Nora who laughs, Nora's laughter rings out again, even louder, this time facing Stevens, her pointed little face raised to Stevens, her eyes creased with laughter and what difference does it make to me if Nora's laughing under Stevens's nose? That pinching in my chest, no, no, it's not grief, just a slight clawing at my heart. Aunt Irene hasn't stirred from her chair all night. In the whirling din of the dance you can make out her pale face, her beige dress, without a crease, her expression like that of an owl nailed to the wall. At a certain point Percival began to scream because he thought the minister was going to devour Nora and me, because the minister was kissing us so much and chewing at our fingers, both of us.

All summer waiting for arrivals. Pretend not to be. Shell peas, peel potatoes. Let Stevens appear once again, only once. Let him talk to me once again, touch me with his man's hands, before he goes back to Florida. Above all, let him look at me, let me be looked at by him, the pale light of his eyes shining all over me, from my head to my feet. To see him. To be seen by him. Experience that one more time. To exist one more time, illumined by him, suffused with light by him, once again to become luminous, living matter beneath his gaze. To live! Somewhere, however, perhaps at the bottom of the earth, the order is given for death. My mother and grandmothers moan in the wind, swear that they've warned me. I had only to flee before Stevens even gazed at me with his child's eyes. Those women talk drivel, keep repeating the same thing. Drops of rain on the water's surface, they sink into the black depths of the sea, counsel me henceforth to dwell there with them, to be obedient and not to make use of the tide to return to Griffin Creek. No, no, I'm not the one who decides, it's the tide that carries me along, every day on the shore of Griffin Creek, amid bits of wood, shells, and wrack filled with iodine. No, no, it's not myself, it's desire that pulls me and drags me, every day, onto the shore. I beg pardon of the great liquid women, my mother and grandmothers. A certain summer, a certain face streaming with moonlight at Griffin Creek. Not in the present tense of ramshackle, deserted houses, but in the wild eternity of the earth. I haunt Griffin Creek so that the summer of 1936 will be reborn.

The lamp over the Atkinses' kitchen table is lit. Outside, the storm is raging. Ben and Alice Atkins's entire family sits around the table, which has been cleared. Children and grownups listen to the storm that shakes the house and makes the bricks in the chimney vibrate. Their little cousin Olivia has been with them for several days now. Lifts the curtain at the window. The surf breaks, crashing, on the rocks. Wave upon rumbling wave mounts an assault on Griffin Creek.

Here he is with them, emerging from the storm, eyes red, clothes soaked, drunk on alcohol and sea visions. He pleads with the Atkins girls to go out with him onto the shore. The greatest show on earth.

Let him speak just to me, not to Nora too, as if we were Siamese twins, let his wild gaze light on me alone, rejecting Nora, and I will follow him out of the house, under the blasts of rain, not bothering to put on my coat. Am I the one he calls in that husky voice? Olivia, Olivia, are you coming? Let him call me one more time, once only, from the bottom of his devastated heart, and I'll be on my feet, ready to go, at his side as he staggers and reeks of alcohol. All the voices of my mother and grandmothers take on the clear tone of my aunt Alice, saying she wouldn't let a dog out on such a night.

Let him call me one more time, once only, and I'll no longer answer for myself. He slumps on the table, his head on his arms.

Can't bear my cousin Nora's body any more as she sleeps beside me in her narrow bed. Feel like clawing her to punish her for being alive at this precise moment when I wish I were alone in the world, facing him who draws me into the night.

While she's fast asleep, happy and carefree even in sleep, I lie on the rug at the foot of the bed. For a moment Nora's peaceful breathing and that of her little sleeping sisters lulls me and calms me. The darkness in the girls' room closes in on us like water. Will I sleep now like someone who has a clear conscience and doesn't hear the man who's calling in the tumult of the storm? I'll never know if I'm dreaming. All night a voice prowls around the house, muffled by masses of rain, gusts of wind, half-human and wild. My name shouted into the night: Olivia! Olivia! Ten times I rise, try to see out the streaming window. The water no longer enters the earth, the house seems to float on the water. No one. No one. I must have been dreaming. I'm the one calling out as I dream. The desire of a girl who calls out in a closed room, while her mother and grandmothers grumble all about the house, declaring that this boy is evil, drunk as a lord, saying I mustn't listen to him, that I risk being ruined along with him.

The next morning Stevens, gaunt, his eyes the color of tow, manages to draw from his foggy brain the one indestructible memory of his dark night. He says that all night he felt as if someone was calling him, while on his rocky spur he was subjected to the assault of the unleashed elements and the storm pounding against his temples.

As I am henceforth outside of time, am I to cross over the summer of 1936 in one leap and see again that other storm, the one of October 28? After scouring so long the gray sand beach and the hill with its familiar houses, between Cap Sec and Cap Sauvagine, it was to be expected. There's some risk that I'll alight upon the sandy bottom of the bay, turned over to the tumult of the east wind. Thus memory travels from one storm to the next.

The very strong currents at Griffin Creek depend in general on the tide. In fact, it was the changing tides that brought about the unbelievable October storm.

Groundswell devastated the sand, forming dunes that were swept away at once, hollowing out ravines that were at once filled in. All life or buried death is rooted out, seized, released in the water's furor. The girls sleeping down below, heads in the sand, the stones and mooring ropes for salmon fishing that weigh them down, are subjected to the chaos of currents and swell. Nora, my cousin, my sister, floats underwater, comes back to the shore of Griffin Creek, the people of Griffin Creek recognize her, turn over her remains to the forensic surgeon, then bury them in the sailors' graveyard. While the current drags me out to sea by the hair. The ocean, its bristling green surface, its deep black heart, my bones dissolved like salt, my soul as tiny as a tear in the immensity of the world.

I should not linger in the vicinity of Griffin Creek. The

great violent images I dread may rise up on the shore at any moment. Assail me anew. I must disappear, make full use of my power to slip over the sea at the speed of the wind.

Though I tell myself it's half-past nine by Maureen's big clock and nothing has happened yet on the night of August 31, I distinctly see two girls walking along the road in the white light of the moon. A boy waits for them by the side of the road, posted there like a sentinel. Soon girls and boy form a single compact black shadow on the bright ground. They walk on the road, all three, arm in arm. Nora refuses Stevens's arm. They've already quarreled, the two of them, earlier in the evening. Someone says you shouldn't look at people's faces in the moonlight.

Through the fabric of my coat, the warm pressure of his arm.

Who speaks first of going to the beach?

Let me just raise my head and I'll see his face, the hardness of his bones streaming with moonlight. His lips curled over his teeth in a strange smile. God, am I to die again?

I have only enough time to cover myself in shadow like an octopus in its ink, to escape onto the sea before the return, in all its fury, of the night of August 31, 1936.

Having acquired the right to inhabit the ocean's depth, its utter darkness, having paid my weight in flesh and bones to the fierce luminous fish, a drop of night in the night, neither moon nor sun can reach me now.

LAST LETTER FROM STEVENS BROWN
TO MICHAEL HOTCHKISS

Autumn 1982

I alone hold the key to this savage parade.

Rimbaud

AM I ABOUT to call on you again after all this time, old Mick? Old: you must be old for real now, potbellied probably, flabby at least, with the little laugh lines at the corners of your eyes as deep as furrows. Anyway, who cares; I'll never see you again and I don't know if you'll even get this letter. Besides, I don't need to know if you're still there in your far-off Florida, or somewhere else in vast America. I don't need an exact picture of you, neither young nor old, even in dream, what I need is that notion of peace, that abstraction of happiness that still lingers in my memory when I hear your name, along with a great flat land inhabited by orange trees in flower and fruit. Only once in my life, this peaceful mooring on the shore of the Gulf of Mexico, at 136 Gulfview Boulevard. It was long before the war broke out. And I'd accomplished the greatest act of brutality in my existence long before war broke out.

I escaped from the Queen Mary Hospital after breaking into the pharmacy. Pink pills, green ones, yellow ones, above all white ones, and bicolored capsules. I've what I need to live and to die. Don't worry, old buddy, my war wounds are invisible to the naked eye. No oozing, stinking sores, no stubs bound up like a Jesus. A face as intact as when I came out of my mother's belly, not red at all but rather white, from lack of air, too much Siamese cabbage for supper, the bridge of my nose finely drawn, eyes that have seen it all—in color. It's all down in black and white in my military file.

It comes, most likely, from what my eyes have seen, what my nose has smelled, my ears have heard, my palate has tasted, my hands have done—with and without a gun. A real feast for the senses. Nerves frayed. Reason, which persists when it should have shattered long ago, under the repeated shock of images, odors, and sharp-beaked sounds. Sea birds set free against my skull. Their deafening cries. I lift my arm, they fly away, they cry. I drop my arm on the hospital sheet and flocks of them return and they cry once more, sharpening their beaks against my skull. Crying out with them to cover their din is no solution, it exhausts me and tears me to shreds.

The sister of charity advances down the aisle, handing out tranquilizers. The blue glow of the night light on her icy white uniform. At times the sister of charity bends very low over an invalid's bed, half-opens her bodice, shows her breasts which shine in the night. The man with no hands or arms weeps. The sister of charity consoles him, bends ever lower, brushes the soldier's cheek with her rosy nipples. Puts them right in his face. In his mouth. He sucks gently, shutting his eyes.

When their bodies were torn to shreds they were twenty years old. Were shipped home, taken in hand by society, laid in neat rows of white beds in big bright sterile rooms, growing old like everyone else, drop by drop, day by day, year by year, and nothing around them changes, slack whiteness, save for death which gleans here and there (the neighbor's striped blue mattress being disinfected and rolled up), while the breasts of the sister of charity are gradually drained of their soft, elastic treasures.

I'm not sick. I cry and shout. Tremble and shudder. A sort of secret fever that no thermometer can detect chills me and burns me. Knit one, purl one. I knit like a woman. When a man weeps like a woman, there's no reason for him not to learn to knit. And if I sometimes drop a stitch it's because the idea, only the idea of Griffin Creek, not even a confused image of it or anything visible and recognizable, is passing through my head, like a stray bullet. So many bullets, so much shrapnel whistle through the room, all around the sleeping men, in the silence of the night, landing at times on their chests, digging holes of horror and dream.

I'm intact because I tell you I am. Slipped through the war as if it were a net. Absolutely unscathed. Not the slightest

scar. Only unhinged. Completely unhinged. Subject to attacks of nerves. Tremble and sweat for no reason. My teeth
chatter. Sheets wet with sweat under my shoulders, in the
small of my back. The torture of a rubber sheet. The root
of a cry boring into my chest, an old family heritage no doubt.
Though any reference to my family or to Griffin Creek is
unbearable. Yell like my brother Percival. Rediscover the
idiot's primal voice. It's the war, old man, only the aftermath
of the war, I tell you, Griffin Creek has nothing to to with it
and neither does my family, which as it happens no longer
exists. Only the frame houses on the hill are still subjected
to the onslaught of wind and salt, graying and falling into
decay, like the abandoned nests of gannets. At least that's
what I heard from a traveler returning from there. Haven't
been back to Griffin Creek myself. Out of the question. Not
a word from any of them since I left. The army, especially
the war, wipes out everything so you start over, from scratch.
Put to sleep by force, awakened by force, calmed down by
force, excited by force, taken in hand, mothered and drugged.
Pills and shots just as the terrors are getting ready in the
shadows. I've nothing to worry about, no cause for complaint.
A late pass from time to time. Comrades with visible battle
scars, myself fit as a fiddle, we veterans stroll up and down
St. Catherine Street, in the east end because it's more fun.
Boys and girls look more and more alike. After following so
many faded jeans, so many bums that are more or less curvy,
it's hard to be sure of anything. Things aren't as clear-cut as
they used to be. Before, you'd have known right away if it
was a boy or a girl, just by watching them shift from foot to
foot. Late pass. If you watch their bottoms closely enough
you can usually tell. The girls generally don't need much
coaxing. Too fast, too eager, too young: I can never go all
the way before I start trembling from head to toe. Aftermath
of the war, old man. Apparitions of fire and sword, great
cries of water birds, screaming girls raped by the light of
fires, the sound of galloping tides. Some day I'll tell everything. Write it all down. The war. More than the war. Everything. That's why I escaped from the Queen Mary. To write
you one long last letter. Without my neighbor's shadow lean-

ing over my shoulder to read what I'm writing as I form the letters. Too crowded there. And then the main ward at the Queen Mary, where for thirty-seven years I've been tolerating the night and the day along with fifty other guys also tolerating the night and the day for thirty-seven years—it's not a healthy way to live. Too many tears and curses leave traces in the dense air. Too many invisible graffiti are inscribed on the walls. It's not worth deciphering other people's despair when you're having trouble breathing yourself, with your heart as big as a millstone in your chest. Create a vacuum inside yourself and all around you. Inhabit a naked space. A sort of blank page and let the words come when I beckon them, to recount the war and all the rest. I wait for them, one at a time, filled with ink and blood, lining up on the page, in order and disorder, only let the words appear and deliver me from my memory. You, who are I don't know where, doing I don't know what, being I don't know what with I don't know whom, maybe you're married, it doesn't matter, I must tell you everything. A long letter written out, page after page, in a schoolboy's black cloth-covered note-book. I bought the notebook and I rented the room.

For some time I'd had my eye on the sign on the Victoria, black letters on a dubious-looking white background over the front door. A dirty brick dump, up here out of the way on Côte des Neiges, backing on the mountain (where the fine houses of Westmount hide among the trees), facing the big park where the dead sleep. "Bachelor apt. for rent." That gave me an idea. As soon as I'd left the Queen Mary, with my black notebook, my razor, my toothbrush, and my supply of pills, I moved into the Victoria. The pills set out in front of me on the plastic table, imitation wood. I look at them for reassurance. I touch the bottles and boxes. I've what I need to live and to die, I tell you. What more can I ask for? It's a matter of helping myself, advisedly. A scant few hours after my arrival I realized I'd have to reverse the order established in the hospital if I wanted to achieve my goal. Upset my habits of thirty-seven years. Change the order of the world to a degree. Take amphetamines at night, barbiturates in the morning. Now that I'm alone I have that power. I use the day and night at my convenience. I wait all day for the noise in the houses to die down to the last din of flushing and faucets, to the TV's last yap. Utter silence in the sleeping house. I concentrate on my writing. Summon the demon to my notebook, if that's what the spirit urges. Use the necessary words. Employ my sweet native tongue for that purpose. This letter I'm writing you, old Mick, will be crammed with obscure information and brief appearances.

The city rumbling under my windows. I look at the black shadow of the elms in the cemetery across the way. Dazzling white headlights, the red lights on the backs of cars. Côte des Neiges stretches out like a long luminous serpent.

No longer to see the city by night. No longer discern the least sigh in the sleeping house. No longer have any present or future. To be merely a man writing in a strange room what his memory dictates. I chew my words like grass, in the manner of cows whose teeth are covered with green saliva. The best thing would be to paint as they taught me to do in the hobby section at the Veterans' Hospital. The truth would show up on my canvas eventually, without my having to describe anything at all. With no one recognizing anything either. I'd create some sort of poisonous flowers, flat on my canvas, with no radiance or odor, just for my pleasure, and that way, old buddy, you'd never know anything.

When I was in the Queen Mary, it wasn't dying that scared me so much as waking up in the morning. To rediscover the horror of the morning among fifty invalids all rediscovering the horror of the morning at the same time. To take up again with your own peculiar horror, to emerge day after day from black limbo, with no images or visitations, all dreams having been smothered by drugs. The head nurse, the one who has the key to the pharmacy, has the power to draw you into the day, to plunge you into the gloom, then haul you out in the morning, your mouth furry, with no saliva and no hope. And if dreams appear in your black sleep they disappear straightaway upon awakening, leaving no trace or memory, as if they'd never existed. The fog you extract from your head in great powdery flakes. The steaming yellow coffee. The daytime pills you swallow. And there you go again. Until tonight. Till the last nocturnal viaticum-valium on your tongue.

The sister of charity has limited powers, aging breasts and drugs that are wearing out. Can no longer protect me from nightmares or my neighbor from watching over his gangrene until morning, without closing his eyes. Men's sobs are more terrible than the end of the world. And yet it's never the end. The world turns on its heel and starts over.

The brown plastic table with veins of darker brown, a poor imitation of the age of wood, has hard, sharp edges, unpleasantly cold to the touch. The row of holy pills lined up carefully on the table before me. Impression of limitless power. Life and death within my reach. Instrument panel. False teak. Control mechanism well in place. Need only stretch out my arm. Hold out my hand. Open the fingers. Let capsules and pearls rain into my palm. Make a fist. Bring it to my lips. Open the fingers. Bring mouth and tongue forward. Like a horse sniffing the handful of oats that tickles his nostrils. Guaranteed odorless, little cold things for life or death. Choose your side. Plug in. If you choose the worst, fill your mouth, your throat. Don't forget the glass of Scotch that facilitates swallowing. Increase the effect. Don't worry, old buddy. Finish my letter first. Won't leave your curiosity unsatisfied. I've sworn I'd tell you everything.

Let sand return to sand, let my gray veins burst on the gray sand of Griffin Creek. That's only wishful thinking. It's in a cardboard room with plastic furniture and a two-burner hot plate that I'll probably end my days. Drained of memory like a disemboweled doll.

The retired salesladies from Woolworth's and Reitman's have turned on their television. Through the cardboard walls you can hear the murmur of half-hearted undressing. The loathsome noise of taps running and toilets flushing resounds in my head. Then all is calm. Some lingering coughs and throat-clearing, irritating as mosquitoes in the dark. The two hairdressers start whispering against the wall. The younger one, the one with the shriller voice, bursts out laughing. His precise words pass through the wall, fall at my feet on the threadbare carpet.

"What a luscious body I've got!"

The night closes around this surprising and cheerful observation.

Wanted so much the silence and dark. Opened the notebook on the table. Shut my eyes. To check out the quality of the silence in the house. Listened for the slightest sound in the street. Beyond the humming motors and squealing brakes, I caught the strange murmur at the city's gates. Recognized savage chirping heading for me. Plead with the void for it to end. For it not to reach me. Now it unfurls above the house. In smaller and smaller circles. The tip of my heart at the very center of the furious sounds. They aim straight at my chest: shall I scream and risk waking the whole house? Better be silent till morning. Go on with my letter as if nothing were happening. Pretend to ignore the flapping wings clattering all through the room. Roof and ceiling open now, burst by tough beaks.

What I have to do, what I've sworn I'd do is beyond my power. To tell you the truth, old Mick, the whole truth and nothing but the truth. I'd rather reach out my hand to the salutary tablets on the table before me. Be done with it once and for all, under the sea birds' glowing eyes. Chattering snow rains down around me.

The gannet suddenly reduces its speed, half-closes its wings, drops head first, like an arrow, vertically. Doesn't close its wings till it touches the water, sending a shower of foam into the air. I've gazed so often at this splendid bird. Rediscover it now, intact and well drawn. It takes just one overly precise image and the rest will follow, come alive, stick the pieces together again, resume its existence, an entire living country fished up from the depth of the dark water. The natal waters of Griffin Creek stirred up by a flock of famished birds, rises to the surface, spreads out its shores, its sea grass, sheer rocks where wooden stairs once rose, for whale fishing. Then come houses and outbuildings, men and women, children and animals, Noah's ark opens under the water's pressure, lets its male and female cargo slip out onto the hill, between Cap Sec and Cap Sauvagine.

On my feet again in my room in the Victoria. Experienced

my waking stupor through my whole body and my head. Ate ten slices of Kleenex bread, so white it looks blued, gulped down a can of beans without heating it up, drank four cups of Salada tea the color of ink, which sets my teeth on edge. Picked up the black notebook. Thought about you, whom I haven't seen for so many years. And what about the war, old buddy? Did you fight in the old country like the gallant average American you are? Don't expect me to talk about the war. The prewar years will be enough to fill you with horror and estrange you from me forever.

At times I'd swear the Atkins girls are here. Came in who knows how. Having followed me from the Queen Mary to the Victoria. All this time they've been chasing me. Never left me, not even in the old country when the earth was on fire. The worst glow of the fire attracted them, made them appear without warning, gleaming in the burst of the flamethrowers with their little faces too white, their rolling eyes. And yet I threw them in the sea, on the night of August 31, 1936.

During one whole summer their mawkish, disgusting girls' manners, their ready excitement. And I alone can put them in their place. Remember, old Mick, back on Gulfview Boulevard, when the two of us would follow the girls walking alongside the sea, dogging their footsteps, reveling in their swaying thighs, to the point of disgust. Approach them, finally, to laugh in their faces.

Olivia, though, so beautiful and guarded. Grew up too soon. Became a woman like the others. In the course of a single summer. I loved her, perhaps, when she was a child sitting on the sand. Her hair foaming in the light. My father hurtles down the path and swoops down on me, to kill me. My mother agrees he should kill me.

While I go to sleep, I avoid turning toward the wall, for fear of something happening behind my back. The strangeness of the air covers my shoulders right away and I huddle there, fearing the worst. This morning I wanted to face up to things. Identified the shabby furniture, the grimy walls, the leftovers on the table, the wide-open notebook. Several times took the inventory of the furniture and objects, each

time using a questionable technique to try and avoid the new
objects, quite visible in the room. Very quickly, no longer
able to use cunning. The massive window full of water covers
one whole wall. A sort of sealed aquarium. In the motionless
water are objects, not floating but stopped there, fixed, clearly
separate the one from the other. Seashells, starfish, bits of
wood, faded reeds, a woman's belt, a blue bracelet. I'm afraid
the glass will break under the water's pressure. I feel the
tension of the water, its contained violence, inside my head.
Its sudden bursting. No sound of broken glass, however. It's
as if, in breaking, the glass itself became liquid. Water leaks
out all over the room. Sea spray wets my face. Everything
inside the glass is now set free. Deathly salt odor set free in
bursts. The smallest bit of wood comes back to life, is unleashed and whirls in the air. It was only to be expected, the
Atkins girls are there, relieved of the ropes and stones that
had kept them at the bottom. Transformed by an unbelievable energy they accuse me, trailing behind them a whole
flock of restless little figures with a determined expression,
who grow as I look on. Men and women of Griffin Creek,
led by my father and mother, rise up to curse me. Chase me
away from Griffin Creek. In a cloud of sand and stones.

The woman on my left wakes up, moaning, louder and
louder, gradually she forms distinct words, they pass through
the wall, fall in clumps in my room, blossom out in curses
and oaths. Morning. The day is beginning. The Victoria resounds once more, vibrates from top to bottom with coughing
and clearing of throats. The flushing and faucets respond,
from floor to floor. The floor creaks under heavy footsteps.
The first bellowing of the radio bursts out, brisk and resonant. Time to gulp down three white pills with a big glass of
water. I plug my ears with the pillow. Gone till evening,
because of a burial.

Night spreads out once more like a leaden cope, over the
Victoria. Only the humming of cars still goes on, one after
another, along Côte des Neiges. Emerge from black sleep.
No saliva, dry mouth, heavy head, escaped with great diffi-
culty from the void, must force the dose of amphetamines.
Picked up my notebook. Swore I'd tell you everything. Hadn't

expected so much sand in my head. Find everything in the sand, if you just look hard enough. The dry grains rubbed in the palms like pumice stone. Wet sand, darker, almost black, clings to the fingers, slips under the nails. Nothing to fear. The shore of Griffin Creek has been swept by equinoctial tides, year after year, for a long time now. No risk of finding any large empty shells on the sand, the still-warm place of their slight bodies, the exact imprint of their violent death carved into the gray ground. So much wind, so many storms and tangled footsteps have clouded the issue for so long now, erased the night, aglow with moonlight, of August 31, 1936. If I persist in seeing the Atkins girls, thunderstruck at my feet on the sand, myself standing over them, foolish and hollow, empty to the very marrow of my bones, it's because there's no end to my dreaming.

A boy and two girls walk along the road of Griffin Creek stepping over puddles of white moonlight. Who is the first to talk of going to the beach?

Bob Allen has already left for Cap Sauvagine, on the pretext that he'd promised Jeremy Lord's daughter he'd spend part of the evening with her.

They know what that means: the father, the mother, the daughter, the son in a row of straight-backed chairs in the kitchen. The bare bulb dangling from its wire over the table. The harsh light reflected on the oilcloth. The official visit from the boy to the girl's family. A word or two every five minutes. Don't speak to the girl too directly. Squeeze her fingers surreptitiously. The girls here are untouchable until the wedding. My uncle the minister told me. All the trouble stems from that. Might as well have your fun with whores and let the little geese stew in their own juices. For that, Nora will never forgive me.

Here she is walking in front of me. Having vehemently refused my arm. Her funny crocheted beret pulled down over her eye, her loose coat slapping at her shins. She darts onto the path leading to the shore, dappled with moonlight, slight and determined.

Olivia needs a little coaxing, stirred by the beauty of the night it appears, and by the strangeness of the moon. I give her my hand and it seems that I'm taking her with me into a forbidden sphere, drenched with white moonlight and infinite calm.

Soon the softness of the sand, in small flat motionless waves under our bare feet, the soft coolness of the nocturnal sand rises up to our ankles. Gazed out for a long time at the moonlight on the sea. All three silent and still, standing there on the sand in the night.

No use hanging around here, there's nothing but sand as far as the eye can see, a field of gray sand at the edge of the sea, awash in long metallic streaks of moonlight. If any objects have been buried here it mustn't be mentioned to that rat McKenna. Extorted a confession from me. Here he is digging in the sand with his policemen-acolytes. A whole flock of frenzied rodents. A white beret at the end of their pickaxe, a woman's shoe perhaps? My life, rather, in great danger, wells up under the plowshare like a broken clump of earth.

Don't worry, old buddy, it's only the gray sand of Griffin Creek, abundantly spreading between Cap Sec and Cap Sauvagine. Might as well be seeking a needle in a haystack. Nora's running shoe filled with sand, like a buried shell. It's my brother Percival who . . . Can only shout and cry. It's odd, how that child's attached to me. Will never betray me.

What's important, old Mick, is that you read my letter right to the end. You understand. It's as if I was asking you to come along the road with me, till there's nothing at all ahead of me, nothing but the abrupt cliff, the void, the leap into the void. Till then I'll talk to you incessantly, tell you everything, address you as if you were there beside me, listening without judging or blaming, only paying unlimited attention to me, Stevens Brown, lost in the hell of Griffin Creek on the night of August 31, 1936.

Everyone in the area agrees, maintains there was no wind that night, that the sea had never been so calm. Yet I, Stevens Brown, son of John and Bea Brown, I declare that something suddenly broke in the quiet air around us. The flimsy bubble still sheltering us suddenly bursts and all three of us are hurled into the furor of the world.

Nora is the first to turn toward me, shouting insults as if

she took pleasure in covering the sound of the waves. No need to shout so loud, the people of Griffin Creek will say, the sea has never been so peaceful, gentle lapping under the moon, flat calm, great slack sea. As for me, I maintain that as Nora was insulting and abusing me, growing drunk on insults and abuse, the crude vocabulary of the men of Griffin Creek, their brutal anger, suddenly emerging from a girl's mouth, a gust of wind came up over the sea, at the end of the horizon, between Cap Sec and Cap Sauvagine. I felt the menace of the storm inside my very head, pounding against my temples, long before anything was visible in the moonlit landscape. Nora repeats that I'm not a man and that she hates me. She's laughing and crying at once, her white crocheted beret still pulled over her eye.

The wind pulls up their skirts, uncovering their knees. No use contradicting myself on that score and claiming that the air is motionless and mild. Olivia tries to calm her cousin. The wind slaps my face. Its iodine smell clings to my skin. Nora's mouth vociferating within reach of my mouth. Repeats that I'm not a man. Tells Olivia to watch out for me. Throws back her head. Her peals of laughter. Raw desire. My hands on her neck for a soothing caress. Her hysterical laughter under my fingers. This girl is mad. The hard ball of laughter in her throat, under my fingers. Simple pressure of the fingers. She sinks to her knees like a battered ox. Her incredulous eyes roll upwards.

A brief silence. A tiny silence to catch my breath. The peace of the world all around us for a moment longer. The crash of the high sea advancing surges into my head once more. Too much noise and furor ever since childhood, too many equinoctial tides have shaken and tossed me. May he who has sown the wind harvest the whirlwind. Didn't have time to take my pleasure from her. From her furor. From the smell of terror in her armpits. From the girl's smell under her skirt, in the russet hollow of her belly. My hands too fast. Poor little Nora fallen so fast onto the sand at my feet, one leg folded under her. Didn't have time to understand myself. My hands only.

I'd be lying, old buddy, if I didn't stress the fact that long after Griffin Creek I still enjoyed Nora Atkins, my cousin, kneeling before me on the sand. In the London blitz, Norman farms under a hail of bullets, the Queen Mary's pharmacy stench, the girl keeps appearing to me, falling to her knees before me, toppling onto the sand with her woman's desire, her woman's contempt subdued and tamed. Not altogether a woman, nor altogether a child, did I mention it before, that age is the most perverse of all. Her lovely body, her auburn hair, her fresh soul now abused. Her allegiance at my feet. For all eternity. Amen.

I have no time to waste, however. Now here's Olivia kneeling beside Nora, bending over her cousin's violet face, then straightening up, jumping back. Is going to escape me, climb back up to the path, bring everyone out. Grab her by the ankles, bring her down on the sand, lie on her. Her rapid breathing. But where I don't agree with all the witnesses from Griffin Creek, from the biggest to the smallest, is on the subject of the weather that night. All will stress the calm of that night, the absence of wind. And I declare that I experienced a raging storm throughout my shaken and battered body, while Olivia was struggling, sharing with me the same frenzied surf. Throughout this story, I've told you already, you must never lose sight of the wind. From beginning to end. From my return to Griffin Creek in June right up to the night of August 31. And doubtless even further. Back to the source of the wind. Swept away by the squall like a wisp of straw, as far back as I go, to the root of my life, pounded by enormous waves, my salty heart cool and alive, rough-skinned seadog, with my cousin Olivia I roll on the sand of Griffin Creek, both of us imprisoned in a raging typhoon, while around us the bright night breathes its sweet nocturnal breath. I swear it's the wind that pulls up her skirt and draws it over her legs. Somewhere in the storm a sort of unbearable moan. Her skirts flap, rounded as a hoop, and I shove myself inside them like a bee in a peony's heart. Soon she starts to cry out. And the wind covers her cries. I am responding enough to the violence of the wind to cry out in turn. Trusting to the furor of the wind to cover our cries. One could roar out all one's unleashed soul, let all one's blood come gushing out and the wind would blow it all away with its gruff triumphant voice, louder than everything. Wind accompaniment to lift you off the earth. The deafening chirping of birds. There again no one agrees, alleging that the birds are silent at night and nest in the crevices of rocks. And I, Stevens Brown, World War II veteran, having fled the Queen Mary to take refuge in my little room in the Victoria, on Côte des Neiges, I swear that on that night wheeling flocks of sea birds were deployed above three bodies lying on the sand of Griffin Creek. Their piercing cries engraved in my memory awaken me every night, change me into a mass of fish, gutted alive on the gutting tables. And do you really think that amid all that din, Olivia's cries fell like drops of water into the sea? The sea's abyss contains us all, possesses us, and reabsorbs us as we fall with a great booming motion. The sea two steps from us. Waves ten feet high, crests of foam, spattered with salt, a whole transport of seaweed, of rockweed of all sorts, of useless debris polished like stones. The salty spray upon our cheeks, you'd think it was tears. It seems to me that at one point Olivia did begin to weep, exhausted from shouting into the wind. As well implore the vast black sky, with its great passing clouds, while the brilliant moon and all the Milky Way turn the world upside down, hiding like the day, its course now over. The sound of her skirts flapping like clothes on a line. I've never in my life seen a night as windy as this one. The whole soul of the sea rumbles and crackles on the shore, exhales its holy furor, its savage moan. The wind hurtles onto the beach, galloping like a herd of buffalo. The wind on my skin makes me shudder, a host of wet tongues swoop down on my body, licking it, tickling it, making it tremble from head to toe. At my most tender point, my softest, strongest point, a weapon that tenses and the fishy sea conch in the middle of Olivia like deep silt that must be attained at all costs. So much clothing to get through, the wind pulls her skirts down on me. To close myself in with her, in the center of her. And die like that at the heart of that torn and crumpled linen. Penetrate to her very depths. Too much wind. Too many cries. Too much underwear as well. The girls the veterans pick up on St. Catherine Street wear only jeans, tight against their buttocks, with nothing underneath. You just pull down the zipper. While Olivia, on August 31, 1936, disappeared beneath a barrage of underwear and elastic that didn't make things any easier, not to mention her fists and her fingernails that plowed at my shoulders and chest. The real problem was how to immobilize her altogether. To abuse her in peace. Call her a slut. Unmask her, the girl who was too beautiful and proper. By playing angel so much you . . . Make her admit that she's hairy under her pants, like an animal. The hidden flaw in her fine and solemn person, that moist black tuft between her thighs, where I fornicate just as I do with whores . . . The roar of my blood gradually subsides, around us the hum of the world becomes confused, recedes onto the sea, while Olivia's piercing cry rises. The cry under my fingers, in her throat. True, it's too easy. Once already, a while ago. Nora. The source of the cry dwindles into a thin thread. Very quickly Olivia joins Nora at my feet, on the sand of Griffin Creek, where punished girls are nothing more than large recumbent stones.

In the silence that follows I understand right away that the calm of the night, the beauty of the night, have not ceased to exist all this time. Only the roaring of my rage has been able to make me believe the contrary. I know, too, that all that calm and beauty will continue to exist at Griffin Creek, as though nothing had happened.

The peace of the world on the sea, its faint lapping against the small boat, the white moon, while I take my cousins out to sea, weighed down with ropes and stones. Amazement, only amazement, sinks into my chest, like the blade of a knife. Slowly rends me.

Perhaps you won't have the courage to read me through to the end. I hope you do, though, because you must know that I've never loved anyone, not even you, old Mick, perhaps Percival, that other self of mine. I hear him saying that I couldn't have done such a thing. He rubs his woolly head against my hand, says again that I'm good. Mockery and deception. May that child greet me in Heaven. Amen.

P.S.   You may be surprised if I tell you, old Mick, that at the

February 1937 assizes I was tried and acquitted, my confession to McKenna having been rejected by the court and considered to have been extorted and not in accordance with the law.